THE MOON
OF LETTING GO

THE MOON
OF LETTING GO

Richard Van Camp

Enfield & Wizenty
(an imprint of Great Plains Publications)
233 Garfield Street S
Winnipeg MB R3G 2M1
www.enfieldandwizenty.ca

Great Plains Publications gratefully acknowledges the financial support
provided for its publishing program by the Government of Canada through
the Canada Book Fund; the Canada Council for the Arts; the Province of
Manitoba through the Book Publishing Tax Credit and the Book Publisher
Marketing Assistance Program; and the Manitoba Arts Council.

Design & Typography by Relish New Brand Experience

Printed in Canada by Friesens

Fifth printing

Library and Archives Canada Cataloguing in Publication

Van Camp, Richard, 1971-
    Moon of letting go and other stories / Richard Van Camp.

Short stories.
ISBN 978-1-894283-93-9 (bound). -- ISBN 978-1-926531-0-07 (pbk.)

    I. Title.

PS8593.A5376M66 2009   C813'.54   C2009-902497-7

ENVIRONMENTAL BENEFITS STATEMENT

Great Plains Publications saved the following resources by printing the pages of this book on chlorine free paper made with 100% post-consumer waste.

TREES	WATER	SOLID WASTE	GREENHOUSE GASES
10	4,431	269	920
FULLY GROWN	GALLONS	POUNDS	POUNDS

Calculations based on research by Environmental Defense and the Paper Task Force. Manufactured at Friesens Corporation

In loving memory of my grandmother Melanie Wah-shee (1914-2007):

"If there is only one of something, hold on to it, love it and don't lose it."

Table of Contents

HEALING

Show Me Yours...

Saw northern lights last night. Nice and big across the sky: 1:30. Green.

We saw baby ones trying to swim like little faint feathers so we helped them by rubbing our fingernails together and whistling and they swam, boy. The northern lights swam and reached across the sky and it was the stairway to heaven kind, the kind that you can see the spirits of those who have passed on walking up, up.

We now walk around town with our baby pictures taped or glued over the pictures of the saints around our necks with leather ties and so when you see someone with the leather necklace you take your baby pic out and show it to them and they marvel at how beautiful you were when you were new, and they do the same.

And then we praise each other:

Oh you were such a beautiful baby.

Look at the dreams in your eyes.

Oh look at your hair. Just like a bear's pelt in spring.

Oh you are so beautiful. So so beautiful. Have a lovely, lovely life.

That's how it is now.

I am proud to say I started this after everything fell apart. It just happened. I woke up and I was in a bad place with bad people and there was little hope for me and there was my grandfather's leather necklace that the priest gave him with a saint I didn't know and there was my favourite baby picture of me on top of the fridge covered in lint and dust and so I cleaned it and took some glue (that we had been sniffing) and I glued my face over St. What's His Hump's and I wore that necklace, tucked 'er under my shirt over my heart.

Two nights later I got rolled and as Franky and Henry were going through my pockets and were holding me upside down they pulled the necklace out.

Henry stopped and said, "What's this you?"

Franky squinted and dropped me. I told them it was a picture of me when I was a baby. They looked at each other and shook their heads.

"Take it easy."

"As if…."

They weren't mad. They were just, well… I don't know.

They let me go and threw my money back at me. "Go home, Richard," they said. "You're not a man anymore."

"I'm trying to be!" I yelled and walked home, rubbing my jaw, stuffing my pockets back in. I'm trying to be….

Two days later I was walking around looking for smokes when they came up to me with goofy grins on their faces and then Franky and Henry showed me theirs. They did what I did and had MacGyver'd saint necklaces to show their baby pictures. Oh they were ugly babies. Maybe this was why they turned out to be such arseholes, but I showed them mine again and we were just so happy to see each other like that.

"Sorry for the other night," Franky said.

"It's okay," I said. You were ugly babies, I thought, and we shook hands.

Then Harvey and his wife came up to us and said, "Hey what you're doing?"

And we all turned and showed them our baby pictures and grinned.

"How cute!" Cynthia said. "Is that you?"

We nodded like gomers and beamed.

"Oh that is too precious," she said. "Let me take a picture."

So we waited while she dug through her purse. Cynthia's trying to be a reporter so we all helped out. Harvey offered us smokes and we took a break. "Thanks for dancing with my wife," he said and I blushed a little. Harvey doesn't like to dance but his wife can't get enough so when I go to the bar she comes up and we two-step around and holy cow she's a great dancer. She keeps her right arm up and holds my hand just barely and boy we just glide and float around that dance floor like butterflies and Harvey keeps his eye on me like a bull moose and I always go up and shake his hand after and he nods back, not too happy that I can dance like I do with his wife but all the same he's pleased that she's happy and enjoying herself.

I know when I hold her on the dance floor I can honestly tell how much she loves him, how she keeps her wedding ring polished just shiny and I can tell how when she moves that she moves for him and that Cynthia is the best thing that ever happened to Harvey.

So Cynthia came back and took a picture of us smiling, holding our baby pictures up, and it ended up in the paper; then, two days later, people came up to me and showed me their baby pictures around their necks on those leather necklaces and we ooh'd and aaah'd each other and we just could not stop laughing.

Oh you were chubby—wah!

Where did all your hair go, eh?

Even then you were a heartbreaker!

Richard Van Camp

Whites, Natives, Inuit—oh we all laughed together when we seen each other and there are just so many beautiful babies inside us all.

Well now after I got hurt at work everybody who came to see me at my house showed me their baby pictures and I just left mine out on the coffee table and we laughed and laughed, passing them around. That pic of our little pictures in the paper really won the heart of our town, so that's what we do now.

And to my surprise Shawna came to see me. I had no idea she was back in town. I really missed her. How sad: when I'm with someone she's single and vice versa.

So now we finally got our timing right and I held her hand and we walked down to the rocks and we saw the baby northern lights trying to swim and she showed me how to call them.

You can do it!

Give 'er!

Go go go!

And those baby lights, they swam out little by little and Shawna and I rubbed our fingernails together and whistled, and soon we had shadows because the northern lights were so bright. Soon, it was like rolling rainbows across the sky.

"You are so beautiful!" she called and then looked to me. "Did you know it's the exact opposite in Nunavut?"

Even though she had a new kind of haircut, she still had fox eyes. "What's that?"

"They rub their fingernails to send them away."

"Hunh," I said, looking up, starting to shiver but not because I was cold. "Maybe they're just glad that we remember halfway what to do."

"As long as we honour them, hey?" she said. I could tell she was going to be a great teacher. I could tell after she said that, and we walked across town holding hands back to my place. I wanted to tell her that sometimes the night was all I had left of her but didn't. I shaved so I could be soft for her while she sang in the shower and we made beautiful love.

We took our time. We laughed and giggled and joked and kissed and caressed, and then we told each other about our lives and how hard it has been these past few years. We both wondered why the lovers we chose all turned out so mean. I noticed she still took the right side of the bed and had a few new moves but we didn't need to talk about it.

"I missed your hands," she said.

"Yours too," I said. I told her to stick around, to quit leaving town. "You could be the love of my life," I said and she went quiet, running her fingers through my hair. I traced my finger along the scars across her arm where that half-wolf bit her. I'm the only man who's allowed to do that. The birds started to sing so I lit her a smoke and we sat up together. I was about to get us some ice water for Round Two and she said, "Wait."

Then she took her beautiful baby Cree picture and held it up and I put mine facing hers and we kissed....

NDNs

Summer, 2004. We were sitting in the lobby of the Stanton Regional Hospital in Yellowknife, my mother weakened by her operation. Mom was on the second floor of the hospital. My grandmother was on the third floor recovering from her first heart attack. From what the doctors told us, Mom's cancer was the size of a blueberry. We think they got it all. My grandmother, my *ehtsi*, was upset because she wanted to head back to Rae, but since my grandfather's passing it was apparent that she could not live on her own anymore. We all wanted her inside the old folks' home in Rae, not in her old apartment, but there was no room in the main frame so our frustration grew every day.

My grandmother kept saying *I want to go home* very softly in English and this surprised me. I thought the only English she knew was the swears. Nobody knew how old my grandmother was. She had always been ancient. There was no one left alive who could remember her as a young girl. "She was always old," they said.

My brothers and I all wished Mom would have taught us Dogrib when we were kids so we could understand their conversations, because it's all in Tlicho. To speak to my grandparents I've always needed translators. This drove me nuts. It never should have been this way.

Standing outside the hospital lobby was Brody having a smoke. The last time I saw him in Fort Smith, which was Christmas Eve, Brody broke my heart. Brody's got a big belly and skinny legs, like a forty-year-old bloated spider. I didn't know what kind of Dene he was or why he was here.

Grandma and Mom were talking in Dogrib. I was getting bored because I couldn't decipher a word. I looked at Brody. At least he could speak English. I looked at him and shook my head. *Maybe now was the best time to do this.*

I got up and walked outside and approached Brody warily. "How's it going?"

"What are you doing here?" he asked, surprised to see me.

"Oh. My grandma's in the hospital." For some reason I didn't want to tell him about my mom. Probably because I still couldn't believe it.

"Sorry to hear that." He held out his hand.

I shook it once. "Yeah...."

"Yeah," he looked away and scratched his brown neck. "I got an operation tomorrow."

"Oh? Everything OK?"

"Yeah, well, I...." he tried but looked down.

I didn't know what to say. Maybe something in him finally blew and he was dying faster than the rest of us.

"So your granny's going to be okay?"

"Yeah. She had a heart attack but she's strong now, wants to go home."

"Where's home?"

"Rae."

"You're Dogrib?"

I felt his energy change. We were Smithers, fighters, but now was not the time, and I didn't have the strength to start anything here. "Yup. Are you Chip or Cree?"

"Chip."

"The caribou eaters."

"Yup."

"It's funny," I said. "We used to be traditional enemies; now we need each other more than ever."

His energy calmed. "You're right."

"We need each other's medicine, songs, healing."

"Yes."

I felt okay standing there with him. I looked him in the eye. "Do you remember the last time I saw you?"

"No."

"It was Christmas, December 23rd. I'd just flown into town and my brother wanted to go Christmas shopping but didn't want to go alone, so we walked uptown. You were passed out on Ducky's lawn in the snow. You were in track pants and a T-shirt. Puke was all over you."

"No—"

"Yup," I read him. He was going to listen for once. "We called an ambulance but they didn't come. We called the cops but they didn't come. We waited and rolled you on your side. You swore you'd never drink again. I asked you what you'd been drinking and for how long. You said you'd been drinking for two weeks steady and you'd taken pills."

Snow had frozen in Brody's raven-black hair. It was cool out, not too cold, but he'd been lying down for so long that the snow was over him in a light powder. Ducky's family just stared stupidly from their windows. My brother and I tried waving down trucks and vans but nobody stopped for long. When they did, they'd see it was Brody and see the puke and drive off. We'd all seen Brody like this before and nobody wanted to help someone who'd been drinking for years. His vomit was orange. It looked like liquefied meat and I wondered if it was his stomach lining.

"My brother and I carried you across the potato field to the hospital. We couldn't wait anymore. You were shivering and you said your stomach was going to burst out."

My brother put Brody's jacket on him to cover his vomit and we lugged Brody's huge arms around us. We half carried, half walked him to the hospital. Thank God he could help but it took forever for three NDNs—two Dogribs and a Chipewyan, traditional enemies—to make our way to the hospital.

"Ooooh, I'll never drink again. Ooooh, I swear to God," he moaned over and over.

The snow fell, light as feathers upon us; we walked over the frozen earth of where the old hospital used to be. This was earth we'd all been born on before they knocked the old hospital down 'cause of asbestos, but we made it to the lobby and the cops were waiting. The nurses, receptionist and RCMP didn't help us. Nobody helped. They all watched and stared like Ducky's family.

"Bring him," a nurse motioned, "to the examining room." Brody wouldn't fit in a wheelchair—he was too big and his stomach was too bloated—so he motioned for us to help him down the hall. He knew where to go. He huffed and started crying as we helped him. When we got him into the examining room, he collapsed on the table. The nurse came in and spoke to him loud, like an older sister. "How are you, Brody? Drinking again? Okay, what did you drink this time?"

"Everything," he said. "Everything I could."

She grabbed a silver bowl and that's when he started to get sick.

My brother and I left and walked by a constable.

"We tried calling you," I said.

"Oh?"

I stopped. "I asked Ducky's family to call the RCMP because they couldn't get a hold of an ambulance."

"Nobody called me."

"Then why are you here?" I asked.

"What?"

"Why are you here if nobody called you?"

"What's your name?" he asked. He did not like me. I gave him my name. He wrote it down. I didn't care. I used to guard for the RCMP so I could afford the attitude. I walked away, my brother and I shaking our heads. Typical. Typical Fort Smith NDN-hating people. Even the NDNs hated the NDNs sometimes. We walked away and I could smell vomit everywhere.

So, you can imagine how surprised I was to see Brody standing and singing at midnight mass the next night in the front row of the church. He was dressed nice and his hair was combed. He stood straight and he sang to every hymn and prayed along with the priest. He was standing next to a girl I used to go to school with. But she looked weak, like a ghost. What the hell was Norma doing with Brody? Were they family? No way. She was Inuk and he was Dene. Maybe she volunteered at the hospital and agreed to take him to mass.

I was shocked that Brody was standing. How could that be? Where did he get his resiliency? Did he have medicine? I looked at Norma and there were sores all over her face. She looked horrible. I felt sad. She used to be so pretty. This shouldn't be the way it was. She was the best athlete in high school, had put Smith on the map nationally and she always won awards at Arctic Winter Games. How had she come to this?

I had danced with her many times in high school. Her eyes always sparkled and she always kept her hair short. She was very soft spoken. I'd been away for years but I knew she had a child with someone. Where was her baby? What in the hell had happened to her?

I cleared my head and prayed hard for the town, my family, my friends. I prayed hard for everything. During the end of mass when we wished each other peace, Brody walked around like a humble Indian and shook hands. He came up to me and shook my hand. Then I smelled his breath. Vodka. It blew hot and thick around me.

Gross. Booze was his medicine.

Brody was drinking again and yet he moved completely sober. I looked into his eyes and he looked right through me. Like a zombie. There was no realization or recollection at all of what happened a day earlier. Norma didn't move. Still too shy, I guess.

Damned Brody. I was so mad in church that he would drink again after half killing himself that it made my blood fierce for war with him.

Richard Van Camp

The rest of Christmas went fine, went great. Dad spoiled us. My brothers and I laughed. I chopped wood, got strong, breathed fresh air, was around fire again. My folks had split years ago so we made daily phone calls to Mom. Little did we know that the cancer was on its way.

Brody came up to me in the drug store a few days later.

"I need to speak to you," he said.

"Now?"

"Maybe in an hour."

"Okay," I lied. "I'll be here." *Yeah right*, I thought: *promise breaker*.

I left for the Mary Kaeser Library and deliberately let three hours slide. I didn't even walk by the drug store when I went home. Why should I go back to Brody when he's just going to break his word? He can't be trusted. I've seen him drunk my whole life. In fact, I don't think I've ever seen him sober.

Here, our coolest elders and some of our outstanding youth have passed on and the drunks remain, pickling themselves for decades on misery and booze, non-contributors who live while cancer eats good people from the inside out alive. Why? I left Smith for Yellowknife to be with my mom for New Year's and tried to forget everything I saw in Smith.

A few months later, my dad and I were at my grandmother's funeral in Indiana. This was my grandmother on my father's side.

"Oh," he said, on the way to the funeral. "Remember Norma, from Smith. You went to school with her?"

I remembered her at the church with Brody. "Yeah, how is she?"

My dad frowned and made a slitting motion with his finger across his throat.

"No...."

He nodded. "In the hospital. She took her own life."

"Pills or rope?" I asked.

He swung his head back and forth, didn't know.

"She had a girl...." I said.

"She lost the girl to Social Services."

"Why?"

He shook his head. "Crack."

We drove on in silence. What happened? NDNs and Inuit on crack cocaine, no less. Who would have thought? Oh I was mad. The truth was I didn't know the north anymore. I'd lived in BC for so long.

So now here we were, Brody and I, outside the hospital.

"The next time I saw you," I said, "you were at midnight mass, with Norma."

"Was I?"

I nodded. "You stood with her. I heard she took her own life."

He bowed his head the same way he did in church and nodded.

"I don't understand what happened."

"She lost her girl, hung herself in the hospital."

I looked away. *What the hell was she doing with you?* I wondered.

"Sad."

"Yeah."

I could smell the smoke from Fort Smith, a ten-hour drive from Yellowknife. There were forest fires around the town and the wind was blowing north. A ten-hour drive and we could both be at Norma's grave. We watched a Ram 3500 tow-truck drive by.

"You came to me in the drugstore a few days after we took you to the hospital. You said you wanted to talk to me."

He nodded. "I remember now."

"So what did you want to say to me?"

"Why didn't you come back?" he asked.

"I had to go home and chop wood for my dad," I lied.

"When you gotta chop wood, you gotta chop wood."

"Yuh."

"I wanted to say thank you." He held out his hand. I shook it. "Where is your grandmother—can I meet her?"

I was surprised. "Sure."

We went back into the hospital and Brody went humble NDN on us, like in midnight mass, and he was polite as hell. Brody shook my mom's hand, NDN style, once and gently, and then he took my grandmother's hand and she looked way up to him and smiled and then he shook my brother's hand.

My grandfather, Pierre, passed away two Julys ago. We miss him so much and have noticed so much sobriety in our family after his passing. They say the old ones can do more work on the other side and can take a lot of pain and suffering with them when they go.... Maybe he took the pain of our family away once and for all. *But why couldn't he spot Mom's cancer?*

I remembered what my *ehtsi* said the last time we visited her in Rae. My mom translated for her. My grandma said:

"When you lose your husband, it is the most miserable feeling. You sit. You sit. You think of the fights you had. What does it matter now? You say stupid things when you fight. Now, it doesn't matter who won, who lost, who was right or who was wrong. What does it matter now?

"I miss him. I miss cooking for him, making his meals. I miss telling stories to him. I keep thinking he is out visiting or shopping for us and that he'll be home any minute. He could walk through the door any second. But he's not coming back. So I sit. I sit and I wait.

"He came to me a few nights ago, his spirit, and told me to start wearing colours again. I had to move on. He said I had to let go and move on. We will never do those things that we loved to do together ever again. When we got together, we did not have kids for five years because I knew nothing. He had to show me everything because I was a tomboy. He showed me how to cook, how to sew, how to be. Now I sit alone," she said. "Now I sit alone."

Then she burst into tears and we all cried in our own way with her. I remember that beside my grandfather's grave is my cousin's. He took his own life in 1990.

I remember after visiting both graves, a golden eagle flew high above Mom's van. It was so beautiful. I had never seen an eagle fly so hard for so long, alone. We dropped tobacco again.

It flew all the way to Yellowknife with us and we called the eagle Grandpa, *ehtse*. I was in awe of the power of our family.

I was in awe of how polite Brody was right now, talking and laughing with my mom and brothers. The dichotomy of drunks has always floored me: how beautiful and pathetic they can be.

Well, that was it. Grandma wanted to go back to her room. We said goodbye to Brody. I said I'd drop tobacco for his operation tomorrow, and we said goodbye. I looked at my mom. I'll never forget how scared we were when we had to say goodbye to her before she went for her operation. To think something the size of a blueberry had brought us all to this. We then escorted my grandmother up to her room. "I want to go home," she said in English.

We'd brought her a bucket of KFC to cheer her up. As we got her settled, I thought about how my grandmother had her own dog team when she was fifteen, and ran twenty miles in one day in snowshoes she'd made herself to go get chewing tobacco for her mother! I saw her now as the last in the line of ancient royalty for our family as she made the sign of the cross three times before the bucket of KFC and got to work....

Dogrib Midnight Runners

I guess how we got this whole thing started was I was sitting at the trailer one night thinking about Justin, thinking about his life. There was this article they ran in the Community News a few years back where his folks announced that Justin had graduated with honours from Aurora College in Yellowknife. There was a picture of him smiling away with his big glasses and puffy hair just as proud as could be, and I remember raising a glass for him. Even though I never went away for schoolin' or ever really travelled, I remember feeling happy that someone was putting Fort Smith on the map.

It was then that I remembered something funny about Justin, the one thing that puzzled me about him: when Justin had a little too much to drink, he loved to streak. That's right. He'd get a glow on at the Buffalo Lounge, go into one of the stalls, take off all of his clothes except his socks, runners and glasses. He'd put his clothes, wallet and belt into a Northern bag and leave it for Country, the bouncer, to come get after Justin made a run for it.

And he'd run, boy. Justin'd run naked through the bar with the biggest smile on his face and everyone would start whooping it up and clapping. The guys would shake their heads and the women would stand to get a good look at him. I only saw him do it a few times but I know he did it quite a bit this past year. The paper ran a few articles on him and they called him The Slave River Streak: "Sources tell the Community News that 'The Slave River Streak' has struck again, running through the potato field last Saturday night at midnight."

Things like that.

One night, me, Brutus and Clarence were cruising around looking for a bush party when we seen this white bum running down the highway.

"Oh God," Clarence said.

Brutus shook his head. "I seen it all now!"

I squinted. Sure enough, it was Justin running down the highway. We all started laughing. Justin was running pretty good—found his groove, I guess. We pulled up alongside him and I was riding shotgun. When I rolled down the window—I'll never forget this—it was a full moon and there was this sheen of sweat on Justin's chest and shoulders. We started whooping it up and calling out to him but he didn't look at us. I seen his puffy hair bob with each bounce and I saw the moonlight shine off his glasses. I never told the boys about this, but when I seen his eyes, I swear to God they were closed. Justin was running blind in the moonlight on the highway outside of town with a smile on his face. It was like a smile you see in church from someone who totally believes. It was a smile that scared me because it was a smile I don't think I ever had or shared. So there we were howling away and Justin kept running....

● ○ ●

His death really hit me hard. I kept thinking, "What broke you, Justin? What could have been so bad that you couldn't ask for help?" I felt for his folks, his woman. I thought to myself, "Let them find peace, Lord. Every single one of them."

I remembered Dad used to say that when the Creator takes a life, he gives two. But what happens when we take our own? It was sad and I couldn't shake it. I thought, "If Justin could kill himself with all he's done in his life, what's to stop anyone else?" He was white, healthy, came from a good family, had money, had Sarah, had work—what could have been so bad?

One night I was sitting home watching TV, sipping coffee and I started to wonder: what was it in the streaking that Justin felt so good about that he'd run with his eyes closed? And what did that feel like—to no longer be able to fight the urge to go for it? What was it like the first time he'd gone for it and made it to the Buffalo Lounge bathroom and dropped his drawers? And what was that first morning after like—opening his eyes and smiling, greeting the day, knowing he'd done it?

It'd been a rough year for me. I just couldn't seem to get on with anything. No job. The thought of one exhausted me. I couldn't stand the thought of making someone else rich or cleaning up after anyone and so every day I'd get up knowing everyone was gettin' paid but me. The past six months I kept saying: "Something good's gotta happen, Lord. Something good. Please."

I thought of Justin again and that smile I seen, and I figured I wanted to try it. What did I have to lose?

I walked out to the back porch of the trailer and took my clothes off. I slowly opened the door and peaked out. In my part of town, at the Caribou Trailer Court, there's starlight like you wouldn't believe. I saw the Big Dipper. Orion. After making sure nobody was around, I crawled naked down my stairs and knelt in my socks and runners. I listened and all I could hear were the rapids far away and my heartbeat racing. "No turning back," I thought. Thank God I had a fence and thank God they hadn't completed the subdivision out back. Finally, I stood and looked around. Then I walked around in the soft grass. "My God," I thought, "there are no bugs." Maybe they were all at the bush parties.

I hadn't run since high school and sure felt it when I jogged around the yard a few times, but I felt good. I felt giddy and light. I also felt more alert than I had in years. I started running a little faster and started feeling a little sexy. I was glad Sheena, my neighbour to the right, and her kids were down south for the summer. My other neighbour—what's her name—had left town and had put her trailer up for sale but, so far, there'd been no takers at all.

So there I was, buck naked—except for my runners and socks—and it was a beautiful night. I opened my gate and jogged behind my house to the east side of the trailer park, through the bush trails. I ran there because they hadn't put up streetlights yet. I ran and started to feel really good. Really *spry* as Coach used to say. I started running and that goddamned German shepherd Snoopy, owned by Lucas Spears, come running out growling at me. The first thing I did was freeze and cover my nuts. I guess Snoopy didn't quite know what to do with me. Here was a skinny, out of shape Dogrib standing there, not moving. He come over and sniffed around.

"Hi, Snoopy," I whispered. As far as I could see, all the house lights were off for the whole street. "Good boy. Where's your daddy?" He tilted his head and I reached out and petted him. Pretty soon he was wagging his tail and he followed me back to my house. I went in and shut the door. *Whew*. That was close. Imagine the Community News getting a hold of that one: "Dog bites Dogrib! (The Tlicho was naked to boot!)"

But it wasn't enough. I had a taste of something. I started to feel a glow inside. So I went back outside. Snoopy was gone but the stars were still shining. I wanted to run again. By this time it was 1:30. Monday. A school night. A work night. Families were asleep. The gas station was closed. The only folks out would be the cabbies, the card players and the partiers—and they'd be out at the landslide or in somebody's home.

I listened. No cars. All I felt was the warm breeze and it felt luxurious. This was it. *Now or never*. I gave 'er down the street and, before I knew it, I was streaking through the back roads of town. I stayed by the bushes in case a truck came around the corner or if there were any stragglers coming home from the bar. I guess the good Lord above took a shine to me because there was no one around. I ran for what seemed like a solid hour and felt something soothingly close to peace.

That night, I had the best sleep I'd had in months. I slept so good and woke up buzzed. I even got up and said a prayer.

I prayed for Justin and I prayed for his family. I prayed for his girlfriend and I prayed for my ex. I prayed for my dearly departed parents. I prayed someone special would soon come my way.

That day I went out and started looking for work. I needed to get out of my head, interact, make some dough.

But before I knew it, the day had passed and I was home, had supper, did dishes, put the coffee on. I was re-reading some Stephen King when I felt it: the night was calling me. She was calling me through my open windows. I could hear her in the rumbling of the frogs out past the highway. My blood was humming and I stripped down in my bathroom. I even tried ten push-ups and ten sit-ups.

I went out in the back yard and did ten jumping jacks. I was feeling pretty good. I decided to stick to my trail from last night. I looked around and took off slowly. I felt like a Dogrib ninja in stealth mode. I started picking up the pace, got into a good jog—then something ran up growling behind me. I stopped and covered up. "Oh God," I said. There was Snoopy, right beside me. He come up to me and started sniffing around.

"Good boy, Snoopy. Good boy. Wanna run with me?"

I don't know why I said that, but he went from maybe wanting to bite me to ears up, wagging his tail. So that was how Snoopy and I became running buddies. We ran together for a week and we loved it. Our territory grew each night. We ran from the Welfare Centre to Indian Village. I kept having this urge to do like Justin and run across the potato field because that was the heart of our community. If I could run across there I'd feel pretty good about streaking through the field that most townies walked across every day. It would be my little victory. But no: that would take time and a lot of daring. So Snoopy and I turned around and started running back home. Again, the stars were out and there was that warm breeze. I could hear the rapids far off and wondered what it would be like to run up the landslide on a night when there were no partiers. I was pretty sure that'd feel great, feel wonderful.

I remember Snoopy and I were just pulling up to my house when the headlights hit me. Full force. From what's her name's house. Her parking lot. *Highbeams!* Then I heard laughter. I froze and covered up, having an immediate heart attack. Snoopy bolted home.

"Grant!" Brutus called out. "What in the hell are you doing?"

Clarence was laughing so hard he fell out of the passenger door. "You..." he kept saying, "You shoulda seen...your face...."

I got so mad I gave them the finger with my free hand and stormed inside my house. I was so ashamed for being caught that I took a shower. I was in there for a while.

"How cheap," I thought. "Isn't this typical? You find something that's all yours, that's magic and people come and twist it." Now I'd be the laughing stock of Fort Smith. I was stupid to think I could have something just for me.

After I was done showering, I went into my room and got dressed. There was no way I was going to sleep anytime soon. I got dressed and sat down in the living room. There was a quiet knock on the door. "Go away," I said.

Again, there was a knock.

"I mean it you guys," I said. "Go home."

The door opened and in walked Brutus and Clarence. They were smirking and I gave them the stink eye, shaking my head as I turned up the TV. The boys went to my fridge and opened it up. I stared at the screen and flicked through the channels. Brutus came around the couch and handed me a Coke. I realized how dry I was, so I took it and we popped ours open at the same time, just like always.

We all took long sips and I felt the burn. We always had this contest to see who could chug the longest and it was Brutus who always won. This time it was no different. I came up for air first, Clarence came second and Brutus closed his eyes and downed half the can. After it was done, we all raised our Cokes and thought of the women we wanted most. We'd done this since grade nine. I hit mute and thought of the new Constable's wife.

Now that our ritual was over, Brutus looked at me seriously and Clarence covered his mouth to stop from bursting out laughing. "Grant," Brutus said. "Want to tell us why you're running naked with Lucas Spears's dog?"

Clarence burst out laughing and slapped his knees. "I'm sorry," he kept saying. "You shoulda…you shoulda…Grant…you shoulda…seen your face…when we caught you."

I don't know how Brutus did it but he kept his most serious face on and didn't move while Clarence fell off the couch behind him. And that was when I burst out laughing. I laughed so hard I started rolling around my couch. Clarence would get going and we were practically in sync with our stops and starts. I'd look up and Brutus would be looking at me, breathing through his nostrils, trying not to laugh.

And that only made me laugh harder.

After a while, I sat up, wiped my eyes and put on a serious face.

And then I told them. I told them everything. I told them about Justin and reminded them about catching him streaking that one night out on the highway, and, for the first time in forever, there were no jokes, no sarcasm, no punch lines. The boys listened as friends. It was Clarence who looked down first and started tracing his finger over the lip of his Coke. Brutus looked down second. I realized that this was the first time since Justin's funeral we had been this sombre, and so I spoke about what a great week I'd been having.

"Well that's why we came by," Clarence said. "We haven't seen you around."

"I been looking for work," I said. "I'm feeling good. I wake up and I want more, you know? I'm tired of drinking, being broke, not having a job. I'm tired of being lonely."

Clarence looked at me and looked at Brutus. "Sounds good to me."

Brutus looked at both of us but didn't say anything. He took a sip of his Coke and Clarence and I did the same. After we were done, Brutus raised his can and said, "For Justin."

We raised our Cokes: "For Justin."

"When are you going again?" Brutus asked.

"What?" Clarence and I asked together.

"You heard me: when are you going again?"

I studied Brutus in a glance. He was being serious. "I go after midnight. The bugs die down then and there's a warm breeze."

"Can I come next time?" Brutus asked.

I saw something in Brutus I hadn't seen before. All our lives, he'd had everything I wanted: best Star Wars toys, best bikes, best guns, cool trucks, and, for the first time, he wanted something I had found. He and I had always competed in our quiet way for leadership in our little group and it felt nice to be asked as the boss. "Sure," I nodded.

Clarence looked at Brutus and then he looked at me. "Wait a minute. Are you guys serious?"

I looked to Clarence. Ever since we were kids, Clarence had always puppy-dogged us.

"I'm serious," Brutus said. "I'd like to try it."

"Well, I'm coming too," Clarence said, and he said it like he always had, like a little brother.

"Okay," I said. "But don't tell anyone. Come over at midnight. Tomorrow."

Clarence raised his hand.

"What?" I asked.

"Um," Clarence paused, "does Snoopy have to come along?"

Brutus started laughing. "Why, Clarence? Are you scared he's gonna get hungry for wieners and beans, or what?"

We had a good laugh about that one.

"He's been running with me for a week," I said. "He likes it."

"Can't we do this without him? I mean, what if he gets hungry?"

"Think of him as our little guardian," Brutus said. "We're Dogribs, after all."

That put a nice spin on it. Clarence liked that. So we raised our Cokes and polished them off together.

That was a week ago. And now our ritual is as follows: we gather at my house at midnight, strip down in my porch. Brutus leaves his clothes on my washer. Clarence leaves his clothes on my dryer. I leave my clothes on the water heater. At first, it was funny: all three of us naked in my backyard warming up.

I was surprised that out of all of us Brutus was in the best shape. He traps, hunts—good Participaction, I guess. The first couple of nights Clarence got so thirsty I wondered if he was going to make 'er. But he did. To my delight, we tackled the landslide and ran right by a party in progress (nobody saw, thank God). We even streaked across the potato field. We had contests to see who could touch all four stop signs at the four-way. Guess what? I won!

On our first run together it was Clarence who reminded me of something I had completely forgotten. "Remember Leonard?" he asked.

"Our babysitter?"

"Yeah."

"What about him?"

"Remember that time he told us about his little gang of roller skaters?"

I looked up. "I remember something. Go on."

"He said that he and his girlfriend and a bunch of their buddies would go roller-skating at midnight and they'd all put on that song, *Come on Eileen* by Dexy's Midnight Runners. 'Member?"

"Oh yeah," I said, "and the cops would try and chase them." I had forgotten that part.

That's when Clarence pulled out a CD. "I burned the song. Wanna crank it?"

"Sure," I said. "Put 'er in."

So there we were all getting undressed while singing along to *Come on Eileen*.

It became our anthem. There we'd be: in my backyard with two speakers aimed out my bedroom window: naked, rocking back and forth singing: "Come on Eileen!" And we'd all raise an imaginary glass and say the next line: "And we can sing just like our fathers." Once we were all warmed up, we'd walk out into my driveway and there'd be Snoopy waiting patiently for all of us. We'd all give him a pet and, for some reason, he'd always run beside me. Maybe because I was the founder of our group.

So this was our agreed ritual: Monday night was run-for-your-ex night; Tuesdays we ran for our parents; Wednesdays we ran for everyone in town; Thursdays we ran for our ancestors; Fridays was happy hour—you could run for whoever you wanted; Saturdays was run for no cancer or diabetes; and Sundays was run for the Creator and all our blessings.

Tonight we cranked our anthem as we warmed up and let ourselves out into the driveway. No moon but she was going to be another glorious evening.

"Friday," I said. "Who are we running for tonight?"

"For Beth," Brutus said. "I really screwed her over. I'm hoping she's happy."

"She got married, huh?" I asked. "To that guy in Chip?"

He nodded. "I heard he was a good guy. I hope they have a great life."

I nodded. "Okay," I took a big breath and looked at my buddies. "Well, it's been a week running with you rowdies and I think it's only right that we give thanks to Justin and his family who inspired all of us."

"*Ho*," Brutus said, but Clarence was quiet.

We turned to Clarence and he was looking away. "For Belinda," he said.

"Belinda?" Brutus asked.

Clarence nodded.

I was curious. "Why Belinda?"

"You're in love or what?" Brutus asked as he stretched.

"She's pregnant," Clarence said.

Brutus and I froze. I seen a tear shine off the tip of Clarence's nose.

"What?" I asked.

He nodded. "She told me she was pregnant."

"When was this?" Brutus asked.

I walked over to Clarence. Brutus did the same.

Clarence kept looking down. "She called me this morning."

"I thought she was with Randy," Brutus said.

Clarence shook his head and held his hand over his eyes. "They broke up months ago."

"Holy," Brutus asked. "What you gonna do?"

That was it. Clarence started to cry quietly. I reached out and felt Clarence's back and Brutus did the same. I couldn't look at Brutus because if he was crying, that'd be it. I'd lose it.

"Hey hey," Brutus said. "It's okay, Clarence. We can help you. You made us uncles, buddy." Brutus had tears in his eyes.

"I'm scared," Clarence said. "I'm not ready to be a dad yet."

I blinked my tears away. "Yeah. You're not alone, Clarence. We can help out."

Clarence wiped his eyes. "I don't want to talk about this anymore. Can we just run?"

"Sure, buddy," I said. "Let's go."

Snoopy was sitting on my lawn, waiting patiently for us to begin.

"Ready?" I asked and looked to my buddies.

"You lead," Brutus said.

I nodded. "We can swing by Belinda's house."

Brutus looked down. "Swing is right."

We all snickered. Even Clarence. Snoopy started wagging his tail.

Belinda was west. We'd streak by there later. Tonight, I wanted the highway, just like Justin. Tonight, I was going to tell the boys to run blind. Tonight, I wanted to feel it: sweat on my shoulders, full on filled with peace. Tonight, I wanted to feel it all, just like Justin did. "*Zunchlei*," I said. "Let's go."

So we ran.

MEDICINE

Love Walked In

The horror show began the exact second I told the truth. This was right after Janette came to town. Single Mom. Body of a stripper.

Kevin was like, "Check out the yummy mummy."

"Yeah," I said.

I always thought women with short hair could only ever be cute. I was wrong. She's white, French. She even sparkled in French. Just listening to her in the Northern line-up warmed The Hammer nicely. The prized ivory of a white woman has put me in the worst kind of heat. Then Wendy's masturbation incident happened, and I lost everything around me.

I saw Janette that aft getting out of her car as I cruised down Candy Lane in my Dad's old truck. She saw me. She was playing hopscotch with her girl and smiled as I drove by for the fiftieth time down her street. God Bless Candy Lane. She stopped to pick something up, and it was the way she bent over that got me. Her shorts were so tight they cupped her ass and I could see her pubic mound. I had to keep on driving, pull over by the airport, turn off and empty myself in gushes onto the high grass. I came squadrons.

The school was still closed until they found a new principal, and this was my life: Jonathan hated me. Nobody waved back; the girls I grew up with ignored me. Fuck them all.

Donna kept calling. She wanted me so badly. She had been cute but that was about it. She had let her hair grow, and that sharpened the curves of her cheeks. Her eyes had gotten darker over the years, like her Mom's, and she was still sort of pretty. And she had those tits. Her ass was a little fat and she was short. I couldn't get her legs over my shoulders if I tried. Funny how she fazed me with those words outside the cafe after the showdown with Jon—"You're a hero"—'cause I was anything but....

Janette, for some reason, had chosen Doug the Slug Stevens as her bull. I couldn't believe this. The Slug raped his fourteen-year-old babysitter years back. That's how he lost his kids. How the Slug got Janette was beyond me, but I was gonna sink his fuckin' boat just like I sunk the principal's.

Donna was knocking on my window last night at two. Her folks were Cree and let her run wild, I guess, whenever and wherever she wanted. She did three taps, waited and did three more. I waited until she left and stroked one off for Janette.

In the morning, Mom brought me a CD as I was combing out the back stoop of my mullet. Jonathan and I grew them on purpose because we were holdouts for the '80s.

"What's this?" I asked.

"You tell me," she said. It was a CD case: Samantha Fox's *Touch Me.*

"I don't know," I said.

"Well somebody left it for someone here, and I know it wasn't intended for me—and it better not be for your father."

I opened it up and saw that Donna had written her name on the inside sleeve. "I must have dropped it last night."

Mom looked at me, stared at me actually. Her eyebrows rose, then lowered. She swept the back of her hand with her palm and this was a move she used to make when she still smoked. She was nervous. "We need you to clear out that brush in the back yard. Snow's coming soon and it'll block the skidoos."

I figured we were back to business. For a while there, I knew my folks were worried about me. After the social worker came and the RCMP took my statement, I wouldn't leave the house. No one called. The weight of my own clothes on my body made me feel like an old man, and it felt like someone was doing a handstand on my shoulders, pushing me down. I worked out twice a day in the basement, stayed in my room for hours just listening to Van Halen, The Cult, The Outfield. All I did was read *Playboy* and try to plan my future sex life: sex with Janette, break her heart, then move on, find someone younger for sex in an elevator, the Mile High club, sex in the bathtub, sex in the shower, sex outside, sex in the rain, sex in the snow, sex out at the cabin, sex on the trapline!

These days, the only someone who calls is Donna, but at least I'm out and about. The one good thing that happened—and the only reason I'm out and about—is I got a call from Mr. Henderson aka Boss Hog over at Northern Lights Log Homes.

"I heard what you did," he said. I could hear chainsaws in the background. "I need a log peeler who's willing to work hard before the snow comes. After that, we'll see if we can train you on the crane. The money's okay. I can't compete with govern-ment, but you'll at least learn how to build your own log home. What do you think?"

Mom and Dad were watching me, and I knew Dad had put the word out that I needed an arrow of light to fly my way.

"Sure," I shrugged. "Why not?"

So I worked all day, peeling logs for Boss Hog. The last thing I wanted to do on coffee break or lunch was ask questions or try to learn about building log homes. The first two days I forgot to bring gloves and shredded my forearms peeling the spruce and pine. After a while I didn't feel it much anymore when the bark bit me. The good news was I was doing push-ups and pull-ups when the boss wasn't around and I got tanned at the same time. To my surprise, that Samantha Fox CD was pretty good. I put it on low and got to work. To my even bigger surprise, Janette drove by in the government truck. I pinched my helmet a few times through my pockets so The Hammer'd swell as she drove by.

I stood up and smiled. I had my shirt off and was sweating something fierce. She smiled back when I flexed the pecs and even turned her head to look directly at me when she came by the second time on her way home from work. Nice.

I ran behind the biggest log pile and jacked off in jets to blast a web of fury and hysteria all over the logs behind the woodpile outside the work site. I surprised myself with how great it felt to come, the relief of it all, but the force and burn didn't fade. It just got better and better. I got quite the tool here that'll last me for life and lead me through a field of women.

● ○ ●

Later, at coffee break, I walked into the office.

"Who's Donna?" Boss Hog asked as he looked up.

"A friend," I said, putting my gloves and hatchet away. "Why?"

"Tell her to quit calling here," he said. "She's called twice today."

"You got it," I said, and blushed in front of the guys.

He paused before getting into his big ass Duelly. "She wants you to meet her for fries and a Coke after work."

Harold, Boss Hog's oldest son, grinned. "How 'bout fries and a cock after work?" The crew howled like wolves and I looked away. Goddamn him. Fuck he had a big buffalo head. Why didn't he get his front teeth replaced?

And goddamn that Donna....

● ○ ●

"Don't call me at work anymore," I said on the phone.

"I want to see you," she said.

I was drip drying from the shower. The tan was coming along good. I was trimming my muff with Dad's moustache scissors. I wanted to have the perfect V, like what I saw in Mom's *Playgirl*. "Not a good idea," I said.

"Remember when we used to go out?"
"Not really," I said. "Bye."

● ○ ●

Janette drove by one more time in the government truck checking the mail for the college. There were four roads to the post office. She chose the road that I was always working next to, which was the slowest. Was I imagining this? No. She looked back, waved and smiled. I waved, stepped out on the road, watched her. She tapped her brake lights twice just to let me know that I wasn't imagining us.

I was gonna fuck her so hard it was gonna be brutal....

I re-read all of my Dad's *Playboys*, couldn't find one Playmate that even remotely looked like Janette. Snuck one of Dad's condoms from the bathroom and came back into rubber.

● ○ ●

Donna called during supper, twice. Mom told her to call back after seven.

"Is that Barb's daughter?"

I scooped a big chunk of caribou into my mouth and nodded.

"I always wondered what happened to you two."

"Mom," I said, "we were in grade five."

Dad nudged me under the table with his leg. "You know," and I could tell I was gonna get a speech because he pulled out his favourite toothpick and moved to his chair by the woodstove. "I don't know how they do it in Africa, but here in the north, it's the bulls who pick, hey?"

"Here we go," Mom said and rolled her eyes.

I got up and poured Dad a coffee and made one for myself. I even put on water for Mom's tea. "Go on."

Richard Van Camp

Dad put his coffee on the rocks, by the woodstove. "Love only works if it's the man who chooses."

"Hmph," Mom said.

"Now, Norma, hear me out. If a woman picks a man, it never lasts. It has to be the man who chooses. When a man chooses, that's when love lasts."

"Oh baloney," Mom said.

"Think of the caribou, Norma. It's not the cows who pick. It's the bulls. Think of the moose, the bison. That's nature workin'."

"I chose you," Mom said.

Dad stopped and looked at her, and the house fell quiet. My Dad smiled and reached out, "Norma, you just made my day. Son, disregard everything your old man just said."

They laughed and went for a kiss. I saw the eagle feather quiver that Mom made Dad on their wedding day. It was filled with eagle feathers they'd collected together over the years when they went camping. Then the phone rang. They looked at me. Dad got up.

"I'm not here," I said.

"Maybe it's Jonathan," Mom said. "You never know."

"Yeah right," I said.

Dad answered it. "Hello?"

He listened and covered the receiver: "You here?" and motioned by pointing at the receiver and mouthed: "It's her."

"Nope," I ran my fingers through my hair. "Cruisin'."

● ○ ●

Candy Lane betrayed me that night. The Slug's Chev was parked outside Janette's house. The only light on at 10:15 couldn't have been her daughter's. Fuckin' guy. I revved my motor outside her house. Nothing. I revved it some more until the neighbour's lights turned on and her neighbour poked his head out. I didn't stop. I kept revving again and an outside light popped on two houses down. Just when I thought the motor was gonna blow through the hood her curtains moved. It was Doug. I peeled out and sped away.

● ○ ●

Saw Donna walking down Main Street, swerved down a back road even though we both knew we saw each other. It was true—we did used to go out.

Grade five—she cried at a party and her cousins surrounded me: "You're really mean, you know," they said.

"Mean? Me?"

"You think you're so cool," Dolly said.

"What did I do?"

"Yeah," Jonathan said. "What did he do?"

"Donna likes you, okay?" Dolly said to me. "Are you happy now?"

I knew Donna did. And the whole school did too the day she wrote my initials on her runners where everyone could see. After a week of nagging from all of her cousins, I agreed to go out with her—if she'd just stop crying.

"Okay," I said as we sat on the playground fence. "Here are the rules. If we're going to go out, you can't walk beside me."

"Okay," she said.

"We're not going to hold hands."

"Okay."

I pointed at her. "Ever."

She was smiling, glowing with happiness.

"You can't call my house and you've got to stop crying."

She sniffled. "Okay."

"Okay?"

"Okay."

She tried to touch my hand, but I pulled it away as if burned by water. "I'm not kidding, Donna. That's strike one."

Fuck, I was mean to her. She'd follow me around the playground and I'd shoo her away or ignore her all day. Then she'd cry and I'd have to talk to her. One hug usually made her happy, but then she'd hold on for dear life and I'd be like, "Okay, you can let go. Okay? Okay!" I had to kill it as summer came. Who knew what tourists would be coming for summer vacation bringing their daughters with them?

God, did Donna cry. Her cousins used their bodies to circle and shield her from seeing me. The bell rang and I slunk by. She yelled out to me, "But what was strike two and strike three?"

Her mascara was all over the place. It was too sad to look. I just kept walking. Then the strangest thing happened. She ignored me. Who did she think she was? That summer nobody hot came to Simmer. I'd see Donna in the park and I'd be like "Hi."

And she'd look to her cousin and say, "Did you hear something?"

Dolly popped her gum and was like, "Nah."

The only time she acknowledged me was at the Northern. One time, I was helping Mom shop and I saw Donna with her Mom. While our Moms decided to have a high school reunion in the dairy aisle, I walked up to her. "Hi," I said.

She walked away without saying a word. Her eyes flashed fiercely as she looked away.

"Hey." I followed her but she sped up. I bolted after her and she was trying to hide in the baby food aisle. I had her. And then I said the stupidest line of my life. Right there, across from the Cheez Whiz, I said the stupidest thing I ever could have said and I don't even know why I said it: "Don't walk away mad, okay? Just walk away." I even had my hands out for full effect.

She rolled her eyes and blushed. "Whatever," she said, before walking away.

When I came around the corner, there stood our Moms. I could tell by their eyes that they'd been watching us and were disappointed that I returned alone. How cheap. This had been a set up.

● ○ ●

Donna tapped on my window at three am last night. I was rock
hard and tempted. Gotta cool it with The Hammer. Got raw spots
where I shimmied that sting when it gasped for air. It would
have been a nice night for a walk with her, to talk and stuff, but
I thought it was best not to lead her on.

I couldn't believe she walked all the way across town to stalk
me. That was a lot of pussy power making her do that. I always
wondered what it was like for a woman to feel horny with nothing
to get hard with but their pink erasers. Maybe the pull I felt for
Janette was the same pull Donna felt for me?

● ○ ●

Goddamn that Janette. Stopped cruising down my street at work.
I was desperate all day. Went behind the log pile and measured
The Hammer with a tape measure: a little over seven and a half.
Not growing, not shrinking, just was.

Then—then! I slammed my frickin' thumb with the back of
the hatchet by accident. God, the pain! It throbbed with agony
that did not let up.

"She'll turn black," Boss Hog said at the first aid station, "and
fall off pretty quick."

Harold handed me an ice pack and shook his walrus head. "You
should have a new thumbnail by the time grade twelve starts."

I looked out the window and winced as a new wave of throbbing came for my thumb. At least Donna had quit calling work.

● ○ ●

Just as I thought all was lost, I cruised down Candy Lane and
Janette's car wasn't there. I raced across the potato field and

sped down Main. Sure enough, her car was outside. The Slug's. There. In the car. They were sitting and yelling at each other. The Slug looked like he was barking at her, he was yelling so loud. I cruised by, but she didn't see me. Things were looking up.

● ○ ●

"Dad," I yelled as we cleared the last of the deadfall. "Tell me about Doug Stevens."

Dad turned off his chain saw. "The Slug?"

"Yeah."

"Bad dude. Nasty temper. I told you what he did to his babysitter."

"Yeah."

"He gets a lot of women, that guy."

"But how? Is he rich, or what?"

"No more than the rest of us."

"So why do women go after him?"

"Funny how that works. Women just can't seem to get enough of a mean man. Isn't he seeing that new woman? What is she—French?"

Dad already knew. He and his pallies got together every night at Stan's house and had a couple cold ones. They listened to Waylon, shot some stick. I couldn't wait until the day they invited me to join them for a drink. They knew, I was sure, all about Janette and the word was out, you could bet, that I had it for her something fierce.

"What's it take, Dad," I asked, "to break a woman's grip on a man?"

Dad stopped and looked at me. He looked at my build and read my eyes. "A good fight can settle things pretty quick. Women respect that. But you're a little young for her, don't you think? Why not go for the one who's calling the house?"

I wrinkled my nose. "Too young."

He nodded and said nothing before starting the chainsaw back on and getting to work. Doug was a dirty fighter, mean. I was worried. I knew I couldn't beat him. Fuck, I was only seventeen.

● ○ ●

Last night there was no tapping on my window. As I waited to hear her footsteps on our gravel driveway, I remembered us going out. I'd known Donna since kindergarten. Before we became strangers, she told me she used to wash her hair twice a day. She also washed her socks with bleach so they always looked new. You could smell it. She had always liked me. I couldn't remember her ever having a boyfriend. She left town for a couple years. Her Dad made some great money in Fort McMurray as a carpenter, but I guess they missed Simmer.

● ○ ●

The day Jonathan and I had it out, Donna was working at the Coffee Shop. I went there to talk to Jonathan but I knew the second I walked in the whole place was brewing for him and me to fight. He hadn't cut his hair so that was a good sign.

"Way to go, winner," Jonathan said and pushed me.

"What's up?"

"What do you mean—what's up? I'm not going to Disneyland is what's up. All because of you."

A small group of girls raced from their seats and surrounded us. "Fight! Fight!" they were yelling. The rest of the girls ran outside.

Uh oh, I thought. Once the girls ran outside, there was no turning back. Jonathan shook his head at me because we both knew the girls would lock their arms into the shape of an octagon like in UFC.

"Fuck sakes anyways," he said. "Now we gotta fight."

"Way to go," I said. They'd probably want us to whip our shirts off and fluff out our mullets now. That's the classic in this town. I looked around. Even the adults and the Chinese owners knew there was no turning back.

"All right," Valerie announced as she walked in. "Let's get it on!"

Jonathan stood and we walked out into the bright sunlight and practically half the town was there. The girls had joined arms and they were all grinning. "Fight! Fight! Fight!" Adults even stood outside the post office while trucks slowed down and pulled into the Terminal parking lot. I'd have to fight Jonathan now, and I didn't want to. He had a bad knee from basketball but that was off limits. Maybe his face bone or his bony ribs. The circle of woman power opened to receive us. The girls all started to cheer and stomp their feet. How cheap. I just couldn't even believe this was my life right now.

Jonathan led me right to the centre before spinning around. "Come on, fucker!" he yelled. He whipped off his shirt and fluffed out his mullet! The girls cheered to hysteria and I could tell by his eyes he was really into this now. I couldn't believe he'd turn this into an academy award performance. He tucked his shirt around his belt. I let out my breath and felt ninety years old. "Take your shirt off, Gerald!" one of the girls yelled. And then they all started cheering. "Shirt! Shirt! Shirt!"

I wasn't going to do it.

"Come on, Gerald!" Debbie yelled. "Take that frickin' shirt off and show us what you got!"

The circle quieted for a second. Debbie's brother committed suicide last summer in their basement so even Jonathan looked at me like I'd better.

He lowered his fists. "Come on, Gerald."

Well, geez, I thought. I took off my shirt and all the girls cheered even louder. Even Debbie. They cheered so loud the back stoop of my mullet practically blew sideways. I tucked my shirt into my belt and smiled. This wasn't so bad. I understood why our Dads did this. It was a Simmer mating ritual and our culture all rolled up in one!

"Fluff the mullet! Fluff the mullet! Fluff the mullet!" they started to chant and I shook my head. God, the women of this town were so bossy.

Jonathan motioned that I had to, so I did. I took my time and leaned back like Dog the Bounty Hunter all slow and luxurious. I flicked my back hair out like I was a party on two legs waiting to happen. The girls went crazy and I wondered if this was what it felt like to be one of the Beatles in their prime. The girls were stomping their feet and going bananas over our hair and I caught Jonathan smiling at me. He loved this. Holy cow, his nipples were the colour of Monday morning hickeys. Then his face hardened so I made mine, too.

"I'm gonna down you!" he yelled and there was more cheering. The fight was on now.

But I stood my ground. I planted my feet on the pavement and raised my hands into fists. "Okay, Jonathan. How long have you known me?"

"Too long," he said and spit by my shoe. He gauged the crowd. The electricity was building. Even the bar stars had made their way around us. And they'd want an all-out brawl with bannock slaps and drop kicks.

"Down him!" someone yelled.

"Yeah," another jeered. "Think you're good, Gerald?"

Jonathan was tough, but he wasn't that tough. He raised his fists and started hopping back and forth, just like in grade seven when I had to teach him how to dance. We stood so close I could see the sweat beads he got on his nostrils in gym class. I started reading his eyes to see how far he was going to take this when a girl kicked me hard towards him. I looked back. All I could see were hands and eyes, hair and purses.

"Listen to me," I yelled to the crowd. "The second that fuckin' principal left town is the second he admitted he did it."

"Bullshit! He's embarrassed," someone yelled back.

"So embarrassed that he stole all your money?" I looked to the crowd. "All of yours? Think about it. This guy's an adult, and he left town in the middle of the night—"

"He's our principal," Jolene yelled. "He wouldn't do anything like that!"

"Yeah!" the crowd yelled. "You're just jealous 'cause you didn't fundraise."

"You lazy Dogrib!"

"Frickin' loser!"

Someone spit on my face and I could smell tobacco and coffee and something like fries and gravy in it. Gah! Jonathan and I looked together to see who it was. Whoever it was was hidden behind the wall of people circling us, kicking us together so hard that Jonathan and I had to hold each other up.

"We're not friends anymore," he said. "I thought I knew you, but it's true. You didn't fundraise. You were jealous 'cause we were gonna go to Disneyland and you weren't."

"Punch the back of his head through the front of his face!" a voice yelled and the circle grew quiet.

It was Torchy and his brother Sfen. I didn't even know how they got where they were but they had their leather jackets off and we could see their tattoos and muscles. They were hardened criminals and their eyes were warlike and fierce. How cheap. They were Dogribs, like me, Kevin Garner, and Wendy.

"Come on," Torchy said. "Is this a fuckin' fight, or what?"

Fuck, he looked rough with his crooked smile. I looked and, sure enough, they had their cowboy boots on. Dad told me they stuffed their cowboy boots with lead so they could kick you in the eyes when they got you down. Also, they only looped their belts at the 3 and 9 position so they could whip them out in a knife fight. They had Tonka sized belt buckles, which they sharpened, to aim for your teeth and face.

Once the whole crowd realized Torchy and Sfen were there, everyone broke up and stood still. I saw fear in Jonathan's eyes as he kicked himself back into the crowd, turned, and pushed his way out of the horde.

"Awwww," the crowd yelled. "Fight him, Jon!"

But even that sounded weak.

Torchy started rolling a smoke and Sfen watched me, to see what I would do. It was like he could melt steel with his eyes he was so tough. I felt the cold gob of spit roll to my neck. I turned and walked away. I used my shirt to wipe the saliva off. It was just slimy and I'd probably get TB now. Gross! I was listening for someone to run behind me and try a cheap shot, but then Donna came running beside me.

"Gerald! Wait!"

I didn't stop walking. She held a hot J Cloth to my face and wiped the spit off. She had to hop up 'cause she's so short.

"Hold still," she said, and I smelled dishwashing soap and vinegar.

"Go away," I said.

"You're a hero," she said.

I rolled my shirt on. "Leave me alone."

"No," she said. "I love you."

My eyes bugged as I walked away. "Take it easy," I said.

Janette never cruised by work that day, so I went for a little cruise myself. Told the boss I had something in the mail and there, before my eyes, walked Janette and The Slug holding hands, downtown, together. I drove by, looked back and she looked away. I double tapped the brakes so the rear lights would flare and Doug saw that. Fuck. I seen him turn to her and I knew he knew. Fuck.

Cruised all day with the sun hot on my arms listening to The Cult's *She Sells Sanctuary* and Van Halen. Didn't know what to do. Janette was in his grip and my dog balls were so loaded for her.

Richard Van Camp

I finally admitted it: goddamn this Beaver Fever. I was so fucking lonely and one woman had to be like any other, right? I cruised by Donna's with the Madness feeling me up. The air was sweet with the aroma of leaves freshly burned in the front yards all over town.

Sure enough, there was a pile of smouldering leaves off to the side of their property and two rakes propped against their porch. Donna was sitting out on her deck with her folks. She saw me and sat up. I stopped, waved her over. She looked at her folks and they checked me out. Her Mom wanted to wave but looked at her hubby. Donna's Dad—Ronny? Donny?—I could never remember his name—looked back down at his paper and Mom put her spatula down. They looked at their daughter, but Donna was already on her way over. She was smiling and blushing. I saw those big knockers of hers sway together as she made her way to my truck, and I saw she was wearing moccasins.

"Hi."

"Hi."

"Nice moccasins."

She looked down and I checked her out. "Thank you. My Mom and I made them." I started to harden, just thinking about it. I got brave. "I missed you last night."

She smiled the sexiest smile and looked left. "I didn't think you ever heard me."

I looked away. "I'm playing hard to get."

She laughed and whispered, "You always have. Did you get my CD?"

I nodded. "She's pretty good."

"What's your favourite song?" she asked, and I could tell she was testing me, reading the wind ahead of us.

I thought about it. "That one that goes, 'Baby I'm lost for words.'"

Her eyes brightened. "That's mine too."

"Can I see you tonight?"

I saw a flush at the base of her neck. She had a little fire in her. "Sure."

"Where and when?"

"Meet me at the park at eleven."

She looked at her folks and looked back at me. "Okay."

"Dress sexy," I said, and I was surprised I said it. Both of us were shocked with my hunger. Her mouth parted and she nodded before looking away. She was blushing. So was I. I drove away feeling like Rocky.

● ○ ●

The other good thing that happened occurred on Day Two of being blacklisted: Pops knocked on my door.

"Come in," I said and sat up.

He saw his stack of *Playboy* and smiled. "Good reading, hey?"

I nodded. "I'm learning."

He chuckled. "I know the Posties think we're swingers, but we renew our subscriptions each Christmas. I can't remember how it started, but I couldn't imagine this house without 'em."

I smiled. "Me either."

"You know, son," he said, and there was his toothpick. "I want you to know I am proud of you, and we stand by you. I think you calling social services took courage, and this is a time that will show you who your true friends are. Your mother and I, well...." He put his hand on mine. "You're a man now." He pulled out the keys to his truck and handed them to me.

Surprised, I asked, "What's this?"

"She's yours now. Take good care of her."

I sat up on the bed. Dad's truck—mine?

"She's got four months left on insurance. After that, it'll be in your name. You're in charge of putting gas in her, and she could use an oil change before the snow comes."

I was speechless.

He held out his hand. "Deal?"

I could not believe it. I took his hand. "Deal."

Richard Van Camp

He hugged me and said, "Love you, son."

I felt the tears well up and had to wait a bit. "Love you too."

"Take her for a cruise," he said. "Your Mom's worried sick, and it'll do her good to know you're getting out."

It was ten at night. "You sure?"

He patted my shoulder. "Sure."

Best ride of my life. I put on one of my Dad's tapes: The Outfield's *Taking My Chances*. I crank it as I cruised. Got out. Saw the townies. Rode by Jonathan's. Saw his light on but didn't honk. I bet he was practicing his guitar and listening to The Cult. I bet he was getting his hair cut to betray me even more. We were supposed to grow it out until we graduated from PWS. Cheap.

I missed the way we could just call each other up to call each other down.

"Hello?"

"Hey. I heard you got a big one."

"Uh huh. That's right. How's you doin'?"

"Got a sore cock and a full belly."

"Same, baby. Same."

I thought about how we used to go snowshoeing out by the highway and one of us—usually Jon—would always say, "They say the grandfathers always take care of you when you're on the land."

Then we'd pretend to be Cree and go, "Tapwe. Tapwe."

I drove by the church and shook my head. The truth never set me free. Doubled back and went down the figure-eight loop to the airport and, despite my nervousness, drove down the clutch-my-sack (Raven talk for cul-de-sac) to where the principal lives.

The lone streetlight caught the hood of the truck, and I could see the dents my father couldn't—or didn't mention—from the afternoon Jonathan and I practiced being the Dukes of Hazard, rolling across the hood of the truck in imaginary getaways.

"I'm Luke!" Jonathan slid across the hood.

I did too. "I'm puke!"

We fell on our knees and held our hands out to the spruce trees. "We're the Dukes, and we're gonna plug you through your panties!'

God, we were like eleven years old. Man that was fun. That was the day we tried Red Man chew like old timers, and threw up in the potato field on the way home for supper.

I got out of the truck, pissed on the principal's lawn, gave him the finger. "That's haunted ground now, fucker," I said. "I hope you burn in hell for what you did."

Just as I hopped in my truck and pulled away, the lights caught something and I slammed on the brakes. There. By the picture window. Someone had touched the house with bloody hands. Wendy?

"Fuck," I whispered.

It was the spookiest thing: a single red handprint on the front of the white house.

"Fuck," I said again and drove away.

I swerved to Jonathan's part of town and stopped outside his house, "And fuck you, Jonathan, for not backing me up!" before smoking the tires and racing away.

I saw his bedroom light turn on in the rearview, but nobody ran out of his house. And that was when I saw another handprint in front of Baxter's house. From what I read in the paper, he was charged with molesting kids at his son's sleepovers. He put something in the food. The kids were never really asleep; they were almost unconscious when he played with their bodies. What the fuck was going on?

● ○ ●

Eleven o'clock. On the road. Picked Donna up, and she never looked finer: jean jacket, hair long, tight jeans and new shoes. Perfume in the cab and she couldn't look at me as we cruised down the highway. Was she virgin? I didn't have the balls to ask.

I was thinking about Janette and the Slug. No cars at her house. Or his. Maybe they would accidentally surprise us in their vehicle as they searched for a place to make out.

We drove down the highway to the towers. I pulled up, turned off the truck but kept the tunes running. I'd brought Samantha Fox and I could tell she loved this. I stared straight ahead and felt her huge eyes on me.

"Strip," I said and looked right at her. "Show off for me."

And she did. Right down to her bra and panties. Donna took her socks off and hissed. "The floor's cold."

I winced when I thought about how I should have cleaned the truck out.

"Okay," she said. "Your turn."

I pulled my shirt over my head, unzipped my pants, took them off and kept my Calvin K's on. She was looking at The Hammer straining to get out. People thought I'd banged my share, but I hadn't. Fooled around. Got a sloppy lick from a Hay River girl with carrot shredder teeth, but no pelt.

"I love your lips," she said.

"Take off your bra," I said.

She looked into my eyes. "I always have, Gerald."

I smiled because I felt that and it felt sweet.

"Turn up the heat," she said.

I did and she reached behind to reveal the most beautiful knockers in town: slopers that supported their own weight with a little bit of side swell. Lovely nipples as long as bullets and cookies as big as loonies. "Damn," I said.

She covered her chest. "What?"

"When did you get that body of yours?"

She was horrified. "Why?"

"'Cause you are hot."

She was still frozen but looked down. She cleared her throat. "Since grade ten."

I couldn't believe what a treasure I'd found. I started sudsing up when she asked, "Bring any condoms?"

"No," I said. "You?"

"No," she said. "I thought you—"

Too late. I was so horny I was shivering and started to kiss her. I pulled her panties off and I could feel her skin against mine. She tasted good, smelled great. Before she knew it, I spread her legs and she leaned back.

"If you love me and my lips," I said, "you're going to love this."

I pull my gonch off and there, fully exposed, rose my hot tusk rising—The Hammer.

"God," she said. She couldn't catch her breath.

I smiled. "Yeah."

"You better not give me the dose, Gerald," she said and pointed at me.

"You too," I said and pointed back.

And we burst out laughing. I was surprised at how good she looked naked. I looked at her fur. She was quiet for a bit before she said, "Don't knock me up."

I scooted towards her trying to aim. "I won't."

She gripped me with her hand and squeezed. "No hickeys or doing your business inside of me, okay?"

"Okay."

She guided me into her and I melted with how hot she was inside. Even my toes started to shiver. And I was shameless. I squeezed her tits and ass and burned my mouth through her neck. I gave her monkey bites all over. I scared myself with how ferocious I was and the whole time she loved everything I gave her. I thought she was gonna blow my eardrums she was so loud.

I could not believe what a great body she had.

So this is how it is? I thought as I glided inside her. This isn't so hard. There was a wet burning heat inside of her and every thrust only got us hotter. I thought I was gonna lose it. I was worried I couldn't come but then I thought about Janette. She tightened and tried to kick away. "No! Not yet. Not inside me."

But I only came harder. It came searing out of me so perfectly I even surprised myself by crying out, grabbing her shoulders and biting her neck.

Richard Van Camp

"Fuck sakes," she said and pushed me hard.

"Sorry."

"What the fuck were you thinking? I told you not to!"

"I wasn't—Sorry! Take it easy."

"Take it easy? I'm not on the pill, Gerald."

I looked at her, made sure no one was coming down the road. No romance here.

She got dressed. I got dressed. We argued back to town. I told her I was sorry a hundred times in the longest twelve minutes of my life that it took to get her home.

"I'm not going home like this," she said. "Take me to the gas station. I need to wash up. My Mom'll be waiting for me at the house."

Fuck sakes. I did. I pulled up and she got out before I could say anything. I bought her an Orange Crush and I grabbed a Coke. When the cooler door opened, I caught a whiff of myself and I smelled us together. Sex!

Lisa Snow was working the counter. Her eyes followed Donna, and I just knew she couldn't wait for me to leave so she could call her friends.

"Hey," I said as I put the drinks on the counter.

She nodded, rang it up and looked out the window. "Two-fifty."

I gave her a Loonie and a Toonie. "Keep it," when she tried to hand me back my change. She still didn't look at me. Well, now that I know what to do, I could fuck her next, if I wanted to.

"Loser," she whispered as I walked away.

"No cock for you," I said loud enough for her to hear as I opened the door.

● ○ ●

Donna washed up, came out smelling great with that perfume of hers.

"Sorry," I said.

"I can't believe this," she said and slammed the door. She was really mad. I'd never seen her mad before and it scared me.

"We'll cruise, okay?"

We cruised to the airport, and I felt bad. She didn't deserve that. I put Van Halen on and *When Love Walks In* came on. We were quiet for a bit, both wishing for something neither of us could have.

After a while I said, "Come on now. Don't be like that."

"Do you do this to all your girlfriends?" she asked and looked out her window. She didn't open her Orange Crush.

I didn't want to go for the sympathy vote, but I told her. "That was my first time."

She looked at me. "What?"

I told her again. "Honest. You're my first."

"Stop the truck!" she yelled.

I pulled over and she was hugging me and kissing me all over my face. "Oh thank you thank you thank you," she said. "Thank you, Gerald."

She was happy and I was relieved. "I'm sorry I was rough," I said. "I was just nervous, I guess."

"Be as rough as you want," she said, "I just don't want a baby yet."

She rubbed her tummy when she said that and that scared me. "Me too," I peeped.

"Let's cruise," she said and she was smiling. "First time, huh?"

I blushed. "Yes."

"Honest?"

"Honest," I said. "Don't tell anyone."

"I won't."

I gave her a mean look. "Do not tell your cousins."

She crossed her arms. "I won't."

"You better not." I said, "especially Bonny."

She reached out and touched my dimple, and for some reason we burst out laughing. I felt great. I felt really good.

Richard Van Camp

By then it was midnight. I thought, if I'm going to get it when I get home, I might as well get it good. We cruised around. Did the figure-eight route between Kid City and the airport and we drove by the principal's turn-off.

"Stop," she said.

"No," I said.

She touched my wrist. "Please."

I stopped, backed up, and turned into the clutch-my-sack facing the house. There was that red handprint again. My heart raced wild and I finished my Coke. I pointed to the handprint and she leaned forward. "What is that?"

I shrugged and flashed my brights on it. "Don't know."

"What happened to your thumb?" she asked. "And your wrists. What are they—those marks?"

"Huh?"

She peeled back my sleeves to reveal the spruce gum stains and scrapes from bark bite. "Suicide," I said and she covered her mouth. I burst out laughing. "No. I'm sorry. That wasn't funny."

Her eyes were huge.

"From work," I said. "The bark of the trees slices me up when I pull it off."

"Why are the marks so black?"

"Spruce gum."

She punched my arm. "Don't joke about suicide!"

"Hey," I pulled away. "Sorry. You really make me nervous, you know."

She pulled away from me. "Well so do you."

"Hey," I said softly.

"Hey what?"

I held out my arm and she looked at me. What was that in her eyes—disappointment? She scooted over and I put my arm around her, and it hit me that we were sitting in my truck like every couple in Simmer does when they make it official. My back started to burn. She had clawed me up!

"You did the right thing," she said.

I tried to figure out which room had been Wendy's. "You figure?"
She nodded and leaned into me. "Can I ask you something?"
I shrugged. "Go ahead."
"How did you know?"
I took a big breath. My folks hadn't even asked me this yet. I knew they were biding their time and giving me mine.
"It's okay if you don't want to talk about it," she said.
Her hair smelled nice. "If you give me a sip of your Orange Crush, I'll tell you, but don't tell anyone, okay?"
"Okay."
I took three mouthfuls and handed it back. I couldn't look at her.
"It was Wendy."
"What about her?"
"Well, you know she was slow, hey?"
She nodded.
"Did you know she was Dogrib?"
"No."
"She is. Same as me. In fact, we're probably related. We were at track practice. This was when Jonathan was still my friend. Well, there we were, getting ready for the high jump when Wendy laid down, took off her clothes and started playing with herself."
Donna cleared her throat and put her hand on my leg. I looked at the principal's house and wondered, which room didn't you rape her in?
"But how did you know?"
I looked at those trees. "This may sound sick, but she had a hot body. The boys knew it. We all knew it. The way she was playing with herself...."
She was quiet for a bit before she answered, "Okay."
"Well, she was doing this for show. She was looking at all of us and licking her lips. I don't know where the fuck she got it, but, somehow, she'd smeared lipstick on her lips and was trying to be all sexy, and I could tell this was rehearsed. Like she was trained, you know? And then I saw her toenails."
"What about them?"

I sat up and flashed my brights on that handprint. "They were painted red. Like that."

"So?"

"A sexy, deep red. The kind women wear."

Donna was quiet, giving me the space I needed.

"Did you ever see his wife?" I asked.

"I keep thinking I did, but now I don't know."

"You couldn't miss her. She was two hundred and forty pounds. She didn't wear nail polish like that. She was a Bible thumper, remember?"

"Go on."

"Wendy didn't put that nail polish on herself, and I know the principal's wife wouldn't. He did."

I could tell this scared her and that was why I was telling her the PG-13 version. She sat up and checked to see if the door was locked. "So what happened?"

"I knew, in that second, that he was molesting her. Think about it: they never took her anywhere. They got a big ol' house. When I called social services, the worker came and took my statement. I didn't tell the coach. I didn't tell Jonathan, but a cop car and a social services vehicle in my driveway pretty much alerted the town it was me who had something to do with his little midnight run."

I pointed to the living room window. They left the drapes closed. You could never see into this house, even on a sunny day. "Look at this house. It's like a wolverine den. He can see everyone who's coming down the road, but you can't see in."

I pointed to the fence. "That fucker put fence all round his property, high walls, barricading himself in. He doesn't have any neighbours, so he could be as loud as he wanted. Whatever went on in that house was so horrible, my Dad told me the Sergeant walked out and vomited when they did the raid."

"God," she said. She made a motion like the sign of the cross but stopped herself.

"The sad thing is his wife knew. You didn't see her out in public much, did you?"

"No." She took another sip and leaned over and kissed my cheek before resting her head on my shoulder. "You should be a cop."

I pulled her closer and could smell her shampoo and perfume. That felt nice. "That fucker called the moving company the night I told and paid cash to Bully's to pack and move his entire house in the middle of the night."

"I can't believe his wife stuck with him."

"Stupid white bitch. They were gone before the cops knew what happened."

"At least social services got Wendy before they left."

"Yeah."

The R Rated version was that it was Kevin Garner, Simmer's Dogrib drug dealer, who pointed out the obvious clue: she was shaved bald.

"You better call social services," he said.

"What? Why not you?"

He looked at her and turned away. "You and I both know she couldn't do that to herself. I'm a dealer, Gerald. You call. They'll believe you."

And he walked.

"He stole our money," Donna said quietly.

"Huh?"

"You know how he was going to take all of the students who fundraised to Disneyland?"

"Yeah."

"We raised over eight thousand dollars."

"Were you a part of that? How much did you raise?"

She looked up "Three hundred and twenty-four dollars. My Mom and I baked pies."

"Really? What else?"

"Cookies and cakes."

I smiled, thinking about this. "You bake?"

She smiled. "Of course."

"You a good cook?"

"Maybe."

I got hard again, thinking of her baking with her Mom, maybe listening to country and western and laughing with her ma as her pops read the paper, smiling in the living room. "What's your best dish?"

"Um...pork chops, gravy, mashed potatoes—"

I flew upon her something fierce. Right then and there across from the house. In the truck. Across from the principal's, I had her undressed with me on top in seconds.

"Don't do your business," she kept saying. "Don't you do it."

"I won't, baby," I said.

She gripped my shoulders and pulled me deep into her with her thighs. "I love you, Gerald," she said suddenly.

"Me too," I said, surprised.

"Oh," she shivered as she swallowed me between her legs. "We fit so perfect."

I didn't do my business. Couldn't. But she did. And how. She took all of me. To the hilt.

● ○ ●

Afterwards, we shivered together.

"Wow," she said. "What happened?"

I got embarrassed. "You turned me on, okay?"

"By talking about cooking?"

"Yeah," I said. "Sorry."

She laughed and kissed my forehead. "Well, if that's all it takes, we'll be great."

I kissed her back. This time I kissed her and no one else. I mean it.

We cruised around and she asked, "You lost a lot by telling, hey?"

I nodded. "Jonathan doesn't talk to me anymore. They just can't shake the fact they're not going to Disneyland."

"Think about what he might have done to the students who went," she said.

I looked at her. That's exactly what the social worker said when she came to the house to take my statement and do follow up. "Thank you for saying that."

She kissed me and touched the side of my face gently. "You are a hero. You saved that girl from more rape. The cops'll get him."

We pulled up to her place. "Hope so."

"Call me, okay?" She looked around. "I've lost my sock."

"I will. Sorry I did my business."

"Where's my sock?"

I looked around. "Maybe you dropped it when we were in the gas station."

"Maybe. Just don't knock me up, and thanks for your cherry."

I laughed out of shock and when I looked up I had tears in my eyes. She kissed my neck and then, in the sign of the cross: fore-head, chin, cheek, cheek. We ended by kissing and she walked away. I went home without cruising down Candy Lane. Can't disrespect my woman, hey.

I wondered: Why didn't we do this years ago?

I went to sleep part of the de-virginized club without washing up. In fact, before I fell asleep, I reached down and used my fingers to smell her all over again.

And the smell was animal. I loved it. I sniffed my fingers and smiled before rolling over. Donna Donna Donna, you finally got me. I thought of Wendy, how I used to pass her in the halls without ever looking at her. The only special needs in high school and she had to be Dogrib. The Crees, Chipewyan, Gwich'in, Slavey and whites just loved that. She made me ashamed to be Tlicho, but I was glad I helped her. I hoped she was safe, wherever she was.

● ○ ●

Richard Van Camp

Woke up smiling. Thank you, God, and thank you, Donna. Felt the weight of telling and being banished leave me as I washed myself clean.

Came out of the bathroom and Mom was standing there holding up a sock. "What's this?" she asked. It was Donna's sock. Bleached white but scuffed from the truck's floormats. The one she left behind.

"I went swimming last night," I said. "Gave a friend a ride home."

"I bet," she said and looked at me. "You make an honest woman out of whoever it is you're seeing. Do this right and with respect."

"I just gave her a ride home, Mom."

I was out the door to work before she could ask when I'd be home for supper.

● ○ ●

Worked all day wincing. Donna's claw marks on my back stung the more I worked up a sweat. Janette drove by twice. The second time she cruised by, I walked out to the road and blocked her. She pulled up beside me and rolled down her window.

"Hi," I said.

"Hello," she said.

"I'm Gerald."

Her eyes sparkled. "Hello, Gerald."

"You're Janette. How's Doug?"

"Fine. Why do you ask?"

"He's mean," I said. Her eyes changed. They narrowed and she stared straight ahead. "What do you want?"

"You."

This got her. She looked back at me. "Can I ask how young you are?"

"Going into grade twelve this September," I said.

She was checking out my chest and arms. "So young," she said. "She yours?" she asked and pointed with her chin to Donna walking down the road towards us.

I glanced at Donna quick. I had maybe two minutes to do this. "Nope. Can I ask you something?"

"Better hurry before your lady gets here."

"She's not my lady." I took a big breath. "I got eight inches. How much does Doug got?"

She looked straight ahead again. Why couldn't she be seventeen? I saw the wrinkles on her face, around her eyes and at the edges of her mouth. She looked weathered. The sag of her neck and the back of her hands gave her age away: "He's got a lot more than that, since you're asking." She lit a smoke, squinted and motioned with her chin, "Look, your little honey's waving at you."

I turned. Donna was waving away. There was a wild panic in her eyes. Shit! "She's a friend." I had to hurry before Donna arrived. "Doug raped his babysitter, you know."

"I've been told this by everyone I meet here."

"We're a Block Parent Community."

"They couldn't prove anything."

"No? Then how come his old lady left him? How come he never sees his daughter?"

"Can we change the subject?"

"Can I see you sometime?"

"No."

"Please?'

She looked at me. "This is crazy."

"I'm a great guy," I said, realizing I was burning across my face.

"I can see that," she said. "She's getting closer."

I looked. Donna was running towards us, her little fists and legs just pumping.

"I have to go," she said.

"Call me at my house," I said. "2999."

She looked away, and I shut the door. She drove away. No double tap on the brakes this time. I couldn't believe how old she looked up close and wondered if The Slug thought of her being seventeen again when he was plums deep....

Donna walked up to me, panting. Her cheeks were a scorched red, like how they always were in gym class after running laps. "Who was that? She has a boyfriend, you know."

"I know," I said. "She's just saying hi."

"Well stop it," she said. "You're taken."

"Says who?"

"Me."

I looked away. I blew it!

"Did you like last night?"

"Sure," I shrugged and blushed. I couldn't believe I'd just made a move on a forty-year-old. "It was fun."

"I think it was more than fun. God, I'm sore and covered in hickeys."

How will I ever get out of this? Boss Hog came out of the office and motioned for me to peel more logs.

"I gotta go," I said.

"Can I help?"

I looked at her and was genuinely touched. Here she was wearing a nice white BUM Equipment pullover and I was covered in spruce gum and she was ready to work with me. "No thanks." I looked at her and knew in a second that she was ready to marry me, cook for me, clean the house, have a few kids.

"Can we go for fries and a Coke after work?" she asked.

I thought about this. I at least owed her that. "I can be there at five."

● ○ ●

When I met her, all five of her cousins were there as witnesses. I could totally tell she told them I'd be there. Donna took her

T-shirt off under her pullover. The entire restaurant could see the monkey bites I gave her, and the word was out: Gerald tagged Donna. Film at eleven. Shit. I was a hostage. Janette, save me! Dolly watched me throughout the entire half-hour episode. Suspicious eyes asked, "How long before you hurt her again?"

When I cruised home, there were police outside Janette's house. Cherries were going and everything. Two social services cars were on the lawn. Man, this was serious. I would've pulled over but the road was too skinny. Half the town drove by to get a good filthy look and I had to keep moving or block traffic. I pulled into my driveway and considered walking back to Janette's to find out what was going on. I was trying to think about what to do when Dad pulled up and wanted me to pluck ducks with him.

"Hear the news?" he asked.

I shook my head.

"See the cops outside that new teacher's house?"

"Yeah."

"The Slug strikes again."

"What?"

"Apparently Doug was starting to abuse that French woman's daughter."

Mom hissed when she took her breath in.

"What?"

"Yeah. Apparently he tried something but her girl told on him."

"Where is he?"

"Jail."

"What about her?"

"She packed up and left with her girl."

"What!"

"She's gone, son."

The breath left my body and it was like I was watching TV for the next four hours but staring straight ahead. I went in my room and lay on the floor, looking up. I was suddenly so very tired and I dozed off. When I woke, Mom and Dad were gone with a note.

Gone shopping for grub.

Surprise supper at seven.

Love, Mom.

I looked at the clock on the stove. I had an hour. I grabbed my coat and cruised to Janette's house. I parked down the street and walked back in the grass. No one was around. I went around back and kicked in the door and it was true. All that was left was the furniture.

Upstairs, downstairs, they left traceless. They were gone. Just as I came out of the house, I surprised two kids who went tearing towards the bush.

"Hey!" I yelled and sprinted after them.

They were wearing hoodies and giving 'er, but I kicked the legs out from under one of them and pushed the other one as he ran so he went face first into the willows. Both boys were down and one was crying. I saw blood on their hands. "What the fuck are you guys doing?"

The first boy looked at me and stared hard. "A rape happened here, right? We left the mark." He pointed back to the house and there were red, bloody hand prints all around the house.

"Jesus," I said.

I looked at the other boy who I realized was a girl with sheared hair. She was holding her leg and leaving red marks on her pants. "Did you cut yourselves?" I asked.

The boy and girl shook their heads. The boy pointed behind me. Then I saw the open bucket of paint. I got the goose pimples and remembered the handprints I'd seen around town. "You kids go home. You shouldn't be around a place like this."

"Were you raped too?" the girl asked.

"What?"

"Were you leaving your mark in the house?"

"No—"

"'Cause you're supposed to leave it on the outside or else they won't see."

"Who—the cops?"

"Torchy and his brother."

I helped them both up. "Wait. I don't understand. I'm seeing handprints around town. Are they behind this?"

"We're behind this," the boy said. "All of us. Cops won't do nothing. Parents don't do nothing. Torchy and Sfen are going to do something about it."

"Like what?" I asked.

"Wait and see," the boy said.

I shook my head and remembered Janette and her daughter. "I gotta go, but you kids go home, okay?"

They looked at each other and nodded. I felt spooky, like I'd interrupted something wicked and holy—I didn't know. I left, hopped in the truck and got back to patrolling.

The Cop Shop was busy: two cruisers with their cherries off and CBC North were parked outside as I sped by. I was tempted to just hit the highway, but I wouldn't even have known where to go, and she had a good four-hour head start on me, and what the hell would I even have said?

"Damn," I said and punched the dash. "Goddamn this town!"

I cruised and cruised with a death grip on the wheel. I looked at the clock on the dash and headed for home.

● ○ ●

When I walked in, Donna was at the house. She was helping Mom in the kitchen. Surprisingly, Dad was upstairs watching TV. Mom looked at Donna who was wiping the counter.

"You never told me Donna was the one who was calling."

I looked at Donna. She was blushing and reading my eyes carefully. "I stopped by," she said, "to give you this."

I looked. There was a small bowl covered in Saran Wrap.

"It's yarrow," she said, "for your arms."

"Now that's sweet," Mom said.

I'm stunned. What the hell was going on here?

"You can put it on after supper," Donna said. "It's pretty strong."

I had to look away.

"What do you say, son?" Dad called from the loft.

"Thank you, Donna," I repeated and dipped my head. This was almost great, but Janette was gone. She was gone.

"Well," Mom said, "Supper's ready. We made your favourite." She looked at me. "Steak, mashed potatoes and nibblets with lots of onions."

"That's a lot of food," I said, "for four."

"Oh, we've invited Donna's folks over. It's been years since Barb and I had a good visit."

Whoah, I thought. Wait—

"Is your Dad still a quiet dude?" Dad asked.

"Yes," Donna smiled. "Still quiet."

"He was always like that," Mom said and put water on for tea. "Even when we were in school. I guess he only needs your Mom to talk to, hey?"

Donna was looking at me. Her eyes sparkled. "That's what my cousins say."

I looked at Donna and my folks. This could work, I thought. Sweetness like hers. Kind eyes. And that simple question: "Can I help?" really got me. I suddenly got this feeling like we could do anything together. She had wanted me for a while and now she had me. She was my first and she could take all of me.

I caught Mom staring at me. She swept the back of her hand with her palm and her eyes asked: is this what you want? I looked at Donna who smiled back and wiped her hands on the dishtowel. This could be my life.

"I remember our first supper," Mom said, "we were just starting out."

"You tricked me," Dad called out from the loft, "and now look at us."

"Yes, look at you," Mom said, "a happy, grateful Dogrib man. Now get down here and set the table."

Donna's folks pulled into the driveway. I saw her Mom in the cab, putting on some lipstick, while her father took off his sunglasses. I could tell he wanted to be somewhere else. They were dressed up real snazzy. Her Dad wore a buttoned up cowboy shirt and it looked freshly ironed. Donna's Mom had a suit top on and probably slacks cause she worked for the government. I looked at Donna. She blushed, looking at me, waiting for me to say something. Maybe we can do this, I thought.

"I'll get the door," I said to Donna. "Your folks are here."

"Wait." She put the dishtowel down and walked across the room. She was smiling, looking into my eyes. She brushed by me, took my hand and faced the door. "We should do this together."

And we did.

The Last Snow of the Virgin Mary

The name is Kevin Garner and dealing isn't who I am. It's not who I want to be. But check this out: there are three joints to a gram, ten bucks a joint or thirty bucks a gram. An eighth is three and a half grams. A quarter is five, six, or seven grams depending if you eye it up or weigh it. If you don't have your weights and you're making a deal on the spot, a loonie weighs seven grams. A half-ounce—we're talking dry, fluffy pot here—is two to three fingers. An ounce is four. For wet, stinky, clingy pot, never measure with your fingers as seven grams can look like three. There are always 28 grams on the ounce: 30 bucks a pop. You make 840 bucks if you're not smokin' or spending. A half-ounce is 14 grams. You can usually move it for $200. There are 16 ounces to a pound, eight ounces to a half-pound and four ounces to a quarter pound. A pound, or an elbow, you can buy for $3,400 or more if it's outdoor—that's hydroponic prices. Clients are willing to pay more if it's indoor because it's more potent, more controlled. There are 448 grams in a pound. You can make $13,440 on one pound alone if you sell it by the gram. Do the math. There are some like Stan the Man who can roll a hundred joints from a single ounce—I'm not there yet, but I'm working on it.

I was in the editing suite at the cable TV office. I had the sniffles and I needed my vitamins. A joint laced with a little blow would have been nice. Six smokes left, some ginseng tea. My nose was still dripping from the cold of the hockey arena but

I was pleased. The game was a success. Lots of slashing, high sticking and cross checking to keep the sheep happy.

Hockey's just modern day lacrosse. How come nobody at Hockey Night in Canada talks about that? I'm surprised Don Cherry doesn't say *it's just a matter of time, folks, before players are allowed to kill one another for public spectacle, so just hang in there, eh!*

The first few goals usually tell the tale, but the Spruce Kings lost to Fort Smith. I, nonetheless, shone brighter than a thousand suns. Man, she was cold at the rink.

Torque. Sandy's physics final exam's tomorrow and the kid's stuck on torque. The little guy reminds me of myself when I was that age, and I'm doing my best to nurture and foster. Now torque, as I explained, is the physics of twisting and turning about an axis measured in Newton metres. Christ, I hope he makes it. The hardcore party crowd still doesn't believe I'm trying to change, that I'm serious about declaring the trailer off limits. I had to run there, get my old VCR tapes beside the porn and WWF archives and lock the doors. That Love Shack of mine was trouble and I had to lose it and the porn. If I was going to be a teacher, I needed a place to study, and if I was gonna get Lona, I'd have to prove to her I could change. Tower's not too happy I'm quitting either and I really gotta think about this. I owe him six grand and I got nothing to show for it. I've been evading his phone calls, even his drive-by's. He was the one who spoiled me, shouldn't have given me that kind of freedom. I was the only dealer in town who didn't pay deposits on the fronts 'cause I had the high school crowd. I saved my best for the regulars, saved the lowest quality for the high school. My fellow grads didn't know the difference and, really, what were they gonna say? Who were they gonna tell?

This hockey game means everything. Can't blow it. I got a bag in my packsack, my last ounce on the street. I'm selling out today. All of it. I'm really trying to change. I'm tutoring, laying off the dope and the booze. I've had mine, but it's time to move on. I just gotta be a teacher. Taping and broadcasting this game is my ticket out. When my alarm clock rings in the morning, it might as well be a bugle: I am on a mission and the only thing that's gonna stop me is a bullet from an elephant gun.

Eleven this morning, head pounding, I walked to the college to get the application forms and who did I see? Goddamn-stuck-in-the-80s-Patsy with her bangs-reaching-for-the-moon. Patsy was the college receptionist and had lathered so much gel in her snare wire hair that it looked crunchy. Everybody calls her Skull Face 'cause you can already tell what her skull looks like. Plus she's queen of the camel toes, a yeast infection waiting to happen, so touch my bum already!

"Whatcha here for, Kev?" Patsy asked. Her sweater was smeared with cat hair. I tried not to look so hung over by running my fingers through my hair and smiled. "Application for the Teacher Education Program."

"Sha right!"

I couldn't stop staring at her lemming teeth. "Seriously."

"You want to be a teacher?"

It hit me I hadn't shaved. Good thing I'm gorgeous. "I want to be a teacher."

"How old are you?"

"18."

"You, Kevin Garner, want to teach our kids?"

I massaged my temples with my thumbs. "Can you be funny later and just give me the application forms?"

"Your truck's still parked outside the Terminal and you're here registering for the TEP Program?"

Ah, I thought, every Welfare Wednesday for the rest of your forgettable life, you're gonna be line dancing to the same tunes at the Legion while I'm down south teaching. I remember when Black Fonzy dedicated *Two Out of Three Ain't Bad* by Meatloaf to you on the Saturday Night Request Show and how I laughed my ass off at the both of you. That's all you're ever gonna get outta life: two out of three in everything.

"You're gonna have to cut your hair, you know," she said as she went to get the application. Sure enough there were her camel toes. I was like, "Hello, left camel toe. Hello, right camel toe. There you are. There you are." You could even see them from behind when she bent over. I was like, "Hello, left bumper. Hello right bumper. There you are. There you are." Someone tapped me on the shoulder. It was Mister Chang, the richest man in town. Chinese. He was holding an invoice in his hand. While everybody else in town owed Mister Chang money, I was one of the proud few who didn't. My overhead's low so I got satellite. I don't give a hang about *Friends* and, really, they should tape the next *Survivor* up here 'cause no one would make it, no one at all.

"You want to be teacher?" he asked.

"Yeah, Mister Chang," I wiped my nose with my sleeve. "I really do."

My auntie who abandoned me and moved to Hay River after Grandma passed made him his parka. She owed him eight hundred bucks for an overdue cable bill. No problem. She traded him the parka, and they called it even. Just like that.

"Good decision, school," he said, "Good money. Summer's off. Get to see the world. Help the kids." He looked at me and studied me for a bit before he said anything more. I had sold his son a few grams and maybe he knew it. "You want a job?" he asked.

I thought about it. Me? Buddy, I got so much money I need a brand new truck to get it to the bank—but then I thought, *Wait a minute. Use this. Earn the town's trust. Earn it.* I smiled and said, "Sure."

"Hockey game finals are tonight at eight. Everybody wants to watch. Hay River, Smith, Yellowknife and Simpson. I need someone to tape the game and broadcast it from the office. You do this and you get into TEP I bet."

Mister Chang was right. Not only was I Dogrib, he knew with my past I'd never get into the Teacher Education Program. I figured if people found out I did all the videotaping tonight and co-ordinated showing the hockey game over the satellite station, surely someone at Aurora College—and Lona—and Tower—and Sandy—and that pig Morris would all see I was trying to change my ways.

"So when's the next bash at your trailer?" Patsy asked and I know she did this on purpose to embarrass me.

"Never again," I said proudly. "I'm finished."

"*Wah!*" she said. "Get out of here."

I looked at Mister Chang who smiled and gave me the coolest nod ever. "Let's go get the equipment."

I got the camcorder from the Cable TV studio, got a quick how-to, but I already knew how. I had taped and broadcast the talent show for the past three years, so it was no prob. The only thing is he uses VHS tapes because he's cheap. I had helped Mister Chang hook up the video feed the summer before at the college so the students there could have video-conferencing with other students and instructors across Canada and the north, so he knew I was good to go. I stumbled past my parked truck (*where are my keys?*) outside the Terminal, and ran all the way home before running to school to start tutoring. No snow yet this year. Skidooers are mad. Everyone's got new machines, but no snow to drive on.

Mister Chang gave me twenty bucks for new videotapes but I pocketed it. That twenty covered my application fee for housing. I figured I could record over some tapes from my trailer. I dialed my answering machine from the station and hit my password: 6969. Five messages. Better not be five scores waiting to happen. Sat down. Gathered my vitamins out of my packsack. Pressed play as I gathered my Excaliburs: two saw-blades wrapped with electrical tape. Those were my buddies: red, hot right away.

"Kev, Jazz here. How's your elbow? Doctor says for 3,500 he'll look at it. This Sunday at the Chinese Smorg. Ciao, bro. Don't spank it too hard or you'll get a purple head!—click!—"

Damn. I wrote this down. I told him not to use the phone lines. I told them to use the Saturday Night Request Show tonight. Send out a request to me. I get back to you from the pay phone downtown. An elbow equals a pound. Thirty five hundred for the quality I got. Why not? There's my tuition and then some. Do they really have a Badger on my line?

I popped 1,000 mgs of Vitamin C, 800 I.U.'s of Vitamin E, 250 mgs of Vitamin B12, 1,000 mgs of Imperial Dragon Korean Red Ginseng and two Kyolic Garlics. Guzzled it all down with my last cold Canadian.

Next message.

"Kev, Larry here. What are you burning? Three spot a G-spot or what? Gimme call, you—click!—"

I shook my head. Translation from Larry's Raven Talk: Can you please lend me three dollars so I can take you out for coffee, but I won't have to pay you back because, after all, I took you out for coffee."

Big burp. One last blast with the Excaliburs. No. Not in here. Not in the station. Oh hell. Truly, hot knifing's where it's at: quick, efficient, no smoke wasted. This would be my thirty-third hot knife off the same gram. Right arm, right arm. Doesn't ninety percent of digestion take place in the mouth?

I've been stoned since I was sixteen. Back then it was like get stoned, see what happens. Now it's like make money off people getting stoned and making things happen. I'm paying for it though. How are my fingers? I have started to notice lately that I feel like I'm missing digits. I believe the end plates of my nerves are rusting with THC, and plus my left eye clicks whenever I roll it backwards. The enzymes in my blood that fuel my dreams are working overtime, and my arms fall asleep quicker than normal. When they tingle, does that mean they're dreaming? The dope's finally starting to catch up with me. I noticed a long time ago that those who start smoking up during their growth spurt develop retarded. They can't do small things with their fingers as they get older. They get lazy, lack hope. I started hooting after growing six foot even so I'm okay—or I was. Now I get deja vus all the time and I'm starting to dream: not DREAM dream, but DREAM like the elders. Spooky.

Next message. Lona? Pleeaaassssse....

"Kev, this is Tower. Listen, it's a good day for a ride. We need to talk—"

Fast forward. Sorry, boss. Next. Beep. Lona? Nothing. Then—

"Kevin. This is Constable Morris Spencer here. Just wanted to see if you thought any more of our talk. You can call me here at the detachment. Talk to you soon.—click—!"

Bastard. Good thing no one was here. They'd think I was turning Narc. It was this goddamn cop that was making me change my ways. Morris took me to the cop shop, poured me a coffee I couldn't taste and told me that this was just a talk between Skins (Yeah, right, pig!). Then the bastard took out the infamous Black Book that the cops keep denying they have.

"Kevin," he said, "you know what this is and your name's in it. You're a young man; you don't have a record. We know you're moving a lot of dope for Tower. This is your only warning. I want you to get out of the racket, Kev. Think about it. If there's something you'd rather be doing, you better start doing it now."

"Can I go now?" I asked. What else could I do?

"Can you go now?" He took off his glasses, pressed his fingers into the side pockets of his tired eyes and had a look at what had oozed there all day before wiping it on his pants. "Do you know what a Badger is, Kevin? It's a neat little computer program we have. It shows who Tower calls and he calls you a lot, doesn't he? It shows who you call. It just grows and grows. We find out a whole network every time you make a call or someone calls you. Neat, eh? It looks like a spider web, and when we show it to a Justice of the Peace, it makes obtaining a search warrant a simple process, especially in this town. We've already looked into your bank account, Kevin. The last time we looked you had four grand in your account. Now where did you get all that money from? Yeah, I guess you can go now."

About a small thousand heart attacks later, I croaked, "Good."

No calls from Lona. I get ass cramps just thinking about her.

The *Fort Simmer Journal* did this article on her and talked about how a modeling agency flew her to Edmonton and took her pictures and have already started lining up deals for her. The town calls her "the little Shania Twain" because she's only 5'6", but what a body. A total knockout. I can't believe she hasn't seen through Dean yet, and I kept hinting about that when we talked at the party. The hell with Dean. Is it just wishful thinking or are they drifting? She's always eyeing me up at the bush parties. Cousin or no, what can Dean give her? That yellow-toothed loser. He lives on top of the bar for Christ sakes.

I don't give a hang if he knows Lona and I were together and talked well past midnight, before I scared her away.

Man, what a one-nipple town. I watch the monitor. It's just about half-time.

I can't believe what Black Fonzy said back at the rink.

The Fort Simmer Spruce Kings ran like crippled trees from their dressing room. Their jerseys are white and black. The team was hung over. You could smell it. Wanna whiff? Think of snails in the same shoebox for a month; now multiply that stink by 69. There you go.

When the Spruce Kings got to the ice, they kicked off their skate guards and pushed themselves away. Black Fonzy. He chopped past me on his skates.

"Yo, Kev, Tower's been lookin' for you."

I changed the battery for the camera. "Tower? Yeah yeah. We met."

"You met? He was just here."

What a burn-out. "Yeah, we met."

"Oh." He looked around. "Think you can score me anymore of that Jamaican finger hash?"

Fonzy was centre for Simmer. Players call him The Fist of God 'cause if he checks you, you'll come to about a hundred feet up looking down on your own body. They say it's a lesson from Jesus.

"Naw, man. I quit."

Fonzy's nose bull's-eyed his dopey face. "You're turning Narc on us, or what?"

"I want to get into the TEP program."

"That's funny." He laughed. "You teach? I heard Tower's got some chocolate-covered shrooms. Why don't you score us some and I'll split it. I got fifty."

"I'm serious, man. I quit."

"Gonna join the robots, huh? What about your weights and torch?"

"You can have 'em for eighty."

"Fifty."

"Seventy-five."

"Sixty."

I give him the nod. "Done."

"What about the trailer that cold-hard-hash made?"

"Sellin' it," I told him.

"I can't see this happening," he said and skated away.

"Sheep," I whispered.

That was when a grunge casualty shuffled up to me, looking this way, that way.

"Mister Garner?"

Some kid. I couldn't remember his name. His hair was so slick it looked like he combed bear grease into his mop. Behind him, a Mongolian horde of snow boarders and shithead skaters posed strong.

"Can you sell me a bag?" he asked.

"A bag of what," I looked around. "Chips? How old are you?"

"We got cash."

I was in shock. He was in Sandy's class. "Get out of here," I said. "Go."

He blushed, shrugged, shambled off back towards the stands and spat.

Man, this town is full of decomposers—and Larry—I got no fuckin' use for Larry. He only goes to the college so he can do panty raids in the women's residence. Um, grow up?

"All right Lay-deeeees and Gentlemen," I said clearly again as I track the players, "Welcome to Moccasin Square Gardens. Tonight I, Kevin Garner, am your play-by-play M.C. as Fort Simmer tries to down Yellowknife for the territorial championships..."

I followed the game and cracked the best jokes I know. This hangover meant nothing. It was all resting on tonight. God, I felt it. I was speaking to the communities, but I was really speaking to Lona, Tower and Constable Morris.

Gerald was sitting with Donna and they were holding hands sharing a coffee. It was about time those two hooked up. Gerald actually had a smile on his face and Donna looked proud. Thank God Gerald called Social Services on the principal. I talked with the crowd between periods and asked Sandy what he thought of the game.

"Simmer blew a two goal lead!" he yelled. It wasn't what I was looking for so I asked, "What's your greatest joy these days in our little community?"

The little champ looked right into the camera and said, "You, Mister Garner! You're the best tutor I've ever had!"

Bingo. The money shot. I swear to God everyone around me clapped. Man, I hope the college president caught that, and that's when I knew: it was time to rewrite history.

Back at the techy's desk at the Fort Simmer Cable office. The phone rang. My palms started burning, just like my Grandma's when she knew something huge was going to happen.

"You're amazing, Kevin," Lona said. "Keep up the great work. This is a great hockey game. I'm sorry for what I said Friday night." My little Shania Twain. Brothers of the world, there is a God and His name is love! Maybe in heaven the guitar solos never end and you get the chick you've always wanted.

"Lona," I said. I was feeling so high and so cocky from the game, but I knew it had to be asked. "Thanks for calling. Hey, did you listen to that tape I made you? That first song, it's called *Smothered Hope* by Skinny Puppy. Beautiful, hey? That's the remix, off their Dystemper album. It's rare and precious, is what

I'm trying to say. Like you. I put the Ministry's remix of it on Side B, but I like this one the best—"

"Kevin, we shouldn't be talking."

I took a puff. "Why?"

"You and Dean are cousins. I don't want to cause friction."

My heart had a G-spot right then and there. I had to sit down. There was hope. I blew my nose. "Are you two still going out?"

"He's trying, Kevin."

"Trying?" I stood up. "He's on the road for Tower. That's not trying. We just have to dance once, you and me. I got some new moves that'll make you blush."

"Kevin—"

"Lona," I took a sip and took another puff. "I'm gonna be a teacher, you know, and I'm out of the dealing business as of tonight. Lona, you're the one for me. I swear to God. I'm sorry I scared you at the party. I'm dying to taste you—"

"I should get going."

"What? What'd I say? Look. I want to kiss you. Can I kiss you?"

"What did Dean do to my back?" she asks, and I can tell she's wanted to ask me this since Friday.

"I don't want to scare you. I got a plan anyways, so don't worry about it."

"You're stoned," she said. "Good-bye."

What! The phone rang again. "Lona?"

Someone was laughing. Music was playing. I could hear the hockey game from the Cable office's cheap little speakers here in the editing suite. My hockey game. My hockey game was in Surround Sound from the monitor and the phone. "Kevin?" a voice giggled. "Kevin, this is Aleaha Apples. Come over. We're in room 304. Women's residence. Bring all your dope."

I sat up. "Who is this?"

"Aleaha Apples. We heard you're selling your stash and we'll buy you out."

Shit. "Who told you that?"

"Black Fonzy."

The word was out now. "Who's all there?"

"Us. Come soon." She burst out laughing and hung up.

Hmmm. If I sell out, I'm free. Maybe pay what I make to Tower...maybe.

On the last tape now at Cable TV. Soon the footage will come. Soon. The twenty that Mister Chang gave me turned out handy. Ordered pizza. She's on the way. Forget the student residence fees for a while. I'm celebrating.

Nineteen minutes left on the last tape and Yellowknife, Hay River, Smith, and Fort Simpson are watching. Tomorrow, when I go for a coffee uptown, everyone's gonna know my name.

Last Friday. After the party. With Lona. Lying down with her on my bed. Without warning, I started to cry about my grandmother being gone. Lona wiped my tears away and kissed my neck. She was the first person I ever told about holding my grandmother's hand for five days before she died. I slid my hands up Lona's shirt but stayed away from her breasteges. No way. Slow down, I thought. Earn her. I caressed her back. Her strong, smooth back. She unbuttoned my shirt and ran her hands over me. We were flush faced and shivering, and I was starting to breathe heavy, heavier than her. I told her how I was at the cross-roads, anything could happen. I wasn't so far gone that I couldn't turn it all around. I told her about a teacher I had, Mrs. Stellan. I was thinking about how she always believed in me and, man, when you have that, anything's possible. I was telling her I'd like to be that somebody for those without, and I can empathize.

I then told her about my ability of echolocation.

"What?"

"I lie on my bed, turn the music off, and send my psychic lasso your way. I know where you were Tuesday night."

She smiled. "Okay. Where?"

"The café. You had a coffee and fries with gravy on the side. You then ordered Iced Tea with a twist of lemon for dessert."

Her eyes lit up. "Where was I Wednesday?"

"Your house helping your mom bake bread. You thought about me all day."

Her jaw dropped. "How did you—"

I smiled. "Echolocation. Like bats. I send out my psychic feelers. When I was a kid, I used to walk on the top of the trees outside the house when I dreamed. Now I just send the signals out there, like a slow spell, and I reel it in. My grandma had medicine. Maybe she passed it on to me."

She kissed my forehead. "You're crazy."

"Maybe."

● ○ ●

I put the mix on that I made for her. Whitesnake sang *Still of the Night* and it got to the solo where the violins play together, like bees dancing, and I always get the shivers when I hear it. As more violins escalate, I feel like I'm climbing the northern lights with a peace stronger than Prozac, and I want to lick something and put my fist through glass at the same time.

I never should have told her about my dream.

"Lona," I said. "You know how you want to be a model?"

She nodded and ran her fingers through my hair.

"Well, I had a dream. It was a little freaky but I want to tell it to you. Grandma said if you have a nightmare, you know, see something horrible about a person, you should tell as many people as you can so it won't come true."

I could feel her pull away, but I held her. "What did you see?"

"Lona," I said. "Give me a stack of Bibles 'cause what I saw was your future."

She sat up. I couldn't stop now. "I saw that you and Dean were still together. You were older, maybe eight years from now."

"And—"

"And you've only gotten more beautiful but the thing is—"

Richard Van Camp

"What?"

"The thing is I saw you getting up to say goodbye to him as he went to work and he looked at you with hate in his eyes and said, 'You got uglier today.'"

Lona made a sound in her throat.

"And you believed it."

She looked around for her jacket. "I'm going now."

"No wait. And the thing is I could see something else too. I saw your arms."

Lona stopped buttoning up her shirt. "What was wrong with them?"

"He gave you horrible tattoos so you couldn't model in anything other than long sleeve shirts. It's like he'd stained you, and he—"

"He what?"

"He also knocked out half of your teeth on your right side, so you could never model close-ups, and your back," I stopped. "He—"

She pulled her shirt up over her face and peeked at me through her bangs. "I'm going now. You're scaring me."

I rose with her. "But you can change this. It doesn't have to happen. I've told you: tell everyone. We can break the dream, so it won't come true."

"You mean if I screw you and leave him, it'll be okay."

"No. It's not that. I'm telling you the truth. And your back," I tried, "He—"

"Kevin, don't ever speak to me again."

She left without tying her shoes or pulling her jacket on. At least she took the mix. She left and nothing I could say stopped her from leaving.

It was true, Lona. My cousin's gonna take his time killing you. For years. And he'll do it from the inside out. I never told you I could see your tummy. He'd mauled your stomach with huge bite marks, and I won't tell you what I saw on your back—but we can stop it—or I can—in a few minutes.

In the editing suite, the phone's been ringing steady. I bide my time until the moment of truth. The callers were people laughing hard and thanking me for a great job. I sprinkled an eighth of a gram on tobacco and rolled it up. Voila Cocoa Puff! I love how coke makes a joint sweet. As always, my lips, tongue and gums go numb as a smoke that smells like vanilla surrounds me. It's like watching '70s porn. There were real women then: long hair, natural. And there's kissing. Remember kissing? They kiss in '70s porn and they take their frickin' time.

"You're gonna make a great teacher!" Mrs. Spencer said. "They say the worst students make the best teachers and I believe it!"

What a sheep. Mrs. Spencer taught me kindergarten ages ago and she's still teaching it today.

"Thanks," I said. "How's Adrienne?"

"Twins!" she beamed.

"Glad to hear it!" I hung up. Good thing I banged her before she got knocked up. I hit Line 2.

"Hey, Kev! It's Patsy. You really were serious about being a teacher weren't you? You'll do it! You'll do it!"

The hell with Black Fonzy! I was flying. "Thanks, Skull Face! Two outta three ain't bad!" I took a puff, a swig, a sip, a shot. I popped two little Effy's just to keep things fine. Back on top, baby.

I figured the town knew what a good job I'd done, so I took the phone off the hook. There could be no distractions for what was about to unfold. I lit a smoke. Maybe tobacco was the Devil's hair. Did anyone ever think of that? Did anyone in this town know that the Chinese called TB The Steaming Bone Disease? Who knows? Who cares? Tomorrow, I will be requesting a number of reference letters from key individuals plus working on a five hundred-word essay on Why I Want To Be a Teacher. This I can write in my sleep as it seems my focus has never been clearer. Let the sheep talk amongst themselves. I am going to be a teacher!

Richard Van Camp

"No more Hash Wednesdays!" I jigged. "No more Spring Bakes!" I danced a Spruce King dance, stopping to slap my ass and go "Hoot hoot!"

I did the last of my coke and looked out the window. Hey, it was sleeting and I was glowing—it's wanting to snow! Thank God it was almost snowing in Fort Simmer! I watched it fall and remembered how Grandma always called snow the quietest mass.

Now, for the real reason I agreed to tape the hockey game.

The moment of truth:

After Sandy finished telling the western NWT what a great tutor I am, I turned the camera around to me and said, "Hello party people. This is Kevin Garner. Yes, I know, the contraband kid. I just wanted to take this opportunity to say hi to Lona and my cousin Dean. Dean Meddows, if you don't know, is my cousin. I love him. I really do. The only problem is I'm in love with Lona Saw. Yup, that's right. I'm declaring this here and now."

I stop to wipe my nose with my sleeve. "You see, folks, a few nights ago I had this dream where I saw Lona and Dean together and they were miserable." I wait. "I had this dream Dean was beating on her on a daily basis and he was taking his time killing her, and I had a dream that she was brainwashed into thinking she needed to stay. Well, Lona Saw, you don't have to stay now. You can leave. I don't want you to be beaten. I want you to be a model. Put Fort Simmer on the map. Make us proud. So that's it. Tell everyone about this. Tell everyone that Kevin Garner had a dream in which he saw the future of Dean Meddows and Lona Saw, and it was horrible. It was a slow motion suicide for both of them, even me. So that's it, folks. That's all. I'd like to dedicate tonight's game in memory of my grandma, Ava Snow, who always said, 'Never let go of a dream.' Thank you and *mahsi cho*."

I turned the camera around and got back to the game.

I turned off the monitor and sound. The hockey game resumed, televised and broadcasting.

It was done. Lona, I just rewrote your fucking history via the moccasin telegraph as each townie tells two friends and those two friends tell their two friends. You're free, Lona. If you stay, well, it's your fault now. I tried. When Dean starts in on you, you'll remember me. Besides—and I don't even mean this—I got Aleaha waiting for me in room 304.

As for your back, Lona, this was what I saw: Dean had you convinced you needed to learn about Reaction Time. Every afternoon, you'd sit on the bed and he'd sit behind you. He'd hold a lit cigarette behind you as you stared at the wall. The game was the closer you felt the heat, the quicker you were supposed to move. Would it be today? Tomorrow? Friday? Next week? You never really caught on, Lona, that he could burn you whenever the fuck he felt like it, and you were too slow and too beat to move away anymore.

Now, Lona. How could I think of something that cruel all by myself if I hadn't seen it? And something else: you've got to get away from Dean, Lona. He loves you like two dogs stuck. If you don't, baby, I saw your exit plan. Your suicide note's going to be three pages long. I was shaking. I stood and made a toast.

"One for the road and two for the ditch. Either way, I just rewrote history. Get outta town, Lona. Make us proud."

I cranked Wasp on the ghetto blaster. Blacky Lawless is blaring, "I WANNA BE SOMEBODY! BE SOMEBODY NOW!!" What the—I looked out the window: pitch black, snowing. The sleet has turned to snow! It is officially snowing!

Grandma said when it snows nothing can touch you. No bad medicine. Nothing. Look at the flakes! As thick as tufts of goose down. Wendy, wherever you are. I pray this snow protects you. Lona, baby. You could'a had me. My truck. We'd cruise, shack-up, make love all night. We could watch the snow fall together for the rest of our lives. I've never made love all night with someone. I've never wanted to hold someone so close to me and to whisper their name with love. To feel your hair, to move inside you. Such a beautiful face. I wanted to feel my skin under your nails. You blew it, baby. You're going out with the wrong cousin. With your atrocious perfume and your beautiful brown Metis eyes.

Richard Van Camp

Now Aleaha at the college residence. I didn't know. To be determined....

Look at that snow. Is it the first or last snowfall of the year that the elders call the Snow of the Virgin Mary because Mary called it for the world? Anyhow, whichever it is, if you collect it, melt it and bottle it, drink it or rub it on a wound, it can cure anything. I think it's the first snow, so Grandma's telling me everything'll be okay.

What am I gonna do about Tower? He took me in after Gran passed, gave me the low down in the deadliest house in Simmer. We sat down, had some tea. Stan the Man was there in his flashy suit. I had always seen these guys around town when I was growing up. They were so cool. We listened to some Neil Young, passed a thick fatty around and sipped African tea.

"Sorry about your grandmother," Tower said. "Anything you need?"

I sat up. "A job would be nice."

"Check this out," Tower broke the science of dealing down to me and finished with a simple question. "You in?"

The language they used, the codes, the poetry of it all. I never felt so alive in my whole life. I nodded: "I'm in."

Tower smiled. "This is your Freedom 35 plan, Kevin. I'm going to start you moving quarters. That all right? Stan here will teach you how to use the scales and eye it up. Remember: although the customer is never right, never underestimate one. Most frequent flyers have scales at home and will hunt you down if you screw 'em, so don't. Do it right. Take pride in your work and watch your ass." He and Stan pointed in unison to a sign on the wall that read WATCH THY ASS! before continuing: "If a customer has a great experience with a company they'll tell four to six people. If they're screwed over by a company, they'll tell fourteen to twenty people. Prevention is the key. You keep 'em satisfied, they'll always come back. You got that?"

I never felt so good in my whole life. "I got it, Tower. Thank you for this."

Tower stood up. "We take care of our own. Dogribs are outnumbered in Fort Simmer, and I have great respect for your grandmother. She and my mom were like sisters. We'll work together, right? It's about getting paid."

"And laid," Stan smiled. "Welcome to the club."

Tower shook my hand like a man. Stan, too. That week I made three grand cash. Cash. You're damn rights I felt great. I got my truck within three months and this trailer is already all mine.

Whoah. Two Summits blasted by the building kicking up mud and snow. They were just the first of hundreds of skidoos that would tear this town up for the next seven months. Soon, half this town would be flying through the fields and ditches. Hoo-yah.

There were kids making snowmen though. One shook a tree, dousing himself with snow. The headlights of a car pulled into the driveway. The white palm of the light when it turned the corner caught the houses across the street, grabbed each house and pushed it down. The door opened. Someone sprinted towards the building. Pizza boy: probably Jessie Chaplin, the Chief's son. Third biggest dealer in town. Now that I was gonna be in TEP, now that I had Aleaha waiting for me, he could keep the tip. I pulled out my twenty and opened the door. All I heard was yelling, "Three little pigmies! Three little pigmies! Disconnect! Disconnect!"

"What?" I asked. I didn't understand. The music was too loud. It wasn't Jessie. It was Mister Chang! He slapped me hard across the face, "Turn it off! Turn it off! Turn off the computer! Stop the tape! Stop the tape!"

I was stunned. He flew to the monitor and turned it on. I couldn't believe what I saw. My heart twisted and my stomach sucked it down. Through the smoke. On the monitor. On the monitor that Fort Smith, Hay River, Fort Simpson and Yellowknife were watching, a naked Nurse Nora was chasing three studs with piggy masks on. The men squealed like pigs and I'd never realized until now what a cheap set they'd used. My least favourite '70s porno!

Three Little Piggies.

My ears were ringing louder than they were this morning. The communities were seeing a porno. My porno. How? I couldn't believe it. I'd been playing a porno! My porno. For how long? The nasty-ass porno I thought I lost forever. How the—?

Nurse Nora bellows, "I'll huff and I'll puff and I'll bloww-wwww your house down!"

Wasp was still blaring, "I WANNA BE SOMEBODY! BE SOMEBODY NOW!!"

There was my porno! I had watched this porno a hundred times at the Love Shack. Ron Jeremy was still skinny in this one. He cracked a few good jokes before going to town. "I WANNA BE SOMEBODY! BE SOME—" Mister Chang banged the ghetto blaster off, ripped at the cables, pulled them right out of the console. He's swearing in Chinese at me. At me! His hood slid off his head. He looked at me. His face was red. *"Ho Cha!* Hockey game ended after you made your little speech! I've been calling here for you but you didn't answer!"

My mind was a whirlwind of rate-limiting-steps that began to eat themselves as they swirled and died together. Had I turned the record button off by accident?

My right eye watered as my cheek started to sting and my hands were set ablaze.

"Get out!" he yelled. Spit landed on his wolverine hood. He was waiting for me to respond. I looked at the little red hand of his that slapped me and then to his purple, puckered lips.

Sandy. God. He was watching the game right now, watching it all. Mister Chang ejected the tape and grabbed the twenty from my palm, holding it in front of his face. "Out!" he says. "Get out! I'm gonna lose my license, you sunovabitch!"

The label on the porno he ejected was switched with a blank label. *This was the one.* I was supposed to tape WWF Raw over this one on Saturday.

My head fell back. I felt the cold winter air bathe me from the open door behind, and I used up fifteen minutes of air in the next two seconds. Tomorrow, Black Fonzy—The Fist of God—was gonna be looking for me for calling his old lady Skull Face. Tomorrow the community would be talking about me at the coffee shop. Everyone was gonna know my name. Everyone! I was dead. I was so dead. I felt my rib cage rise and fall as I released a death sigh to the ceiling.

Grandma, you lied. Anything and anyone can get you in the snow....

Who wanted me now—with my horrible night? I had an ounce on the street and a bag in my pack. My name was Kevin Garner. I wanted to be a teacher. I turned and I went, dizzy through the snow as it popped and crunched under my feet. To the women's residence. Aleaha. Tower. Stan. Constable Morris. Bury me deep, somebody, under this snow of deceit....

Sandy—

Lona—

Anyone—

The Moon of Letting Go

Her life was about her son now.

She thought about this after the funeral as she and Robby made their way to the car with groceries. Healthy food for her parents before she drove back to Smith in the morning. She was in Rae, *Behcho Ko*, an hour and ten minutes out of Yellowknife, ten hours away from Fort Smith. This afternoon a funeral for a boy who never woke up. A distant cousin's son. The coffin was tiny. The community was lost in grief.

Robby had been at her side and had been quiet throughout the day.

"How are you?" she asked.

He shrugged. But then smiled. "Happy to be with you, Mom."

He was becoming his father. His smile and charming eyes were the same. He would be tall. Her father had remarked on his feet and hands. Like a pup who'd one day lead. You could tell in the lope and hands.

Behcho Ko was still dusty. The town quiet but with graffiti all over the houses. Tonight a quiet feast with family. Tomorrow the ten-hour drive. It would be good to head back. Since arriving, she'd noticed that nothing but the names had changed: even though they called Rae *Behcho Ko*, and even though the Dogribs were calling themselves *Tlicho*, there was still too much gambling, there were still too many new trucks and empty cupboards. Children played late, late into the evening. There was non-stop bingo. Steady commutes to Yellowknife for bingo. And the drinking. Would it ever end? Where were the parents? "We have a problem with our youth." She'd kept hearing that since she'd returned. She knew it wasn't our youth; it was our parents. But she kept that to herself.

Running her tongue along her chipped bottom tooth, she thought about these things as she put the groceries into the trunk of the car and made her way inside. She got in first. Robby second. She took a big breath and squinted through the spider-webbed window, the dust, when Robby said quickly, "There's an old man in our car."

She looked up and, in the rearview mirror, saw the devil sitting in the back seat. That was what they'd called him all her life. The most dangerous medicine man in the communities. The rattlesnake. "Oh," she said quickly. "Hello, Uncle."

She cursed herself for calling him family but she did it for the boy. She did it for her son. She didn't want him to be scared.

The old man nodded. He'd gotten skinny, she'd noticed. Sitting there in his suit and cap, you'd think he was like any other elder, but you'd know he wasn't. You'd have to. How could you not feel the blackness bleeding out of him.

"Uncle," she said. "I think you are sitting in the wrong car."

"*Ee-le*," he said. "I'm sitting in your car."

Celestine glanced at her son and turned her body, placed herself between them, so Robby couldn't fully turn to see him. Nor could they touch. They mustn't touch, she panicked. *They can't.*

"How can we help you? Do you need a ride?" Again, she cursed herself for speaking quickly without thinking. But it was for the boy, for her son. He mustn't know that within reach, within a quick pluck of a strand of hair, sat the man who could be paid to kill, cripple, or curse someone. Even as a girl, she'd seen half the town—including the priest—cross the street when he approached.

"I want you to drive me around," he said. "Now."

"Oh," she said, looking around, looking for one truck or car she could hand him off to. But who would take him? She already knew. No one. It was a Sunday. The town was quiet, mourning. She glanced towards the lake and saw curtains close from a kitchen window. Who lived there and what had they seen?

"I have to take my son and the groceries home to my parents," she said.

"*Neezee*," he nodded. "Then we'll go."

"I'm staying with you," Robby said and touched her arm.

"Robby," she said but knew not to argue with him. Not in front of the old man. "Robby," she said and reached in her purse for a five dollar bill. "Please go get us a drink. What would you like, Uncle?"

She did this to stall for time. She had to make it clear. She had to say what she needed to say before they went anywhere.

"Orange Crush," he said. This surprised her.

"*Huh uh*," she nodded. "Robby, get yourself a drink, okay? *Ho.*"

"What would you like, Mama?" Robby asked. He never called her *Mama* anymore until now. He must have known. He must have known she was in trouble or in terror.

"Coke," she said. "In a can. Ice cold."

It was going to be a hot day. She couldn't remember the last time she'd had a Coke but she'd need something now, an edge.

Robby was gone but not before touching her arm softly. She nodded without looking at him because she knew if she looked she'd start to shake. To have something so dangerous and close to her son again was something she swore would never happen to them. And here it was.

Robby closed the door behind him and made his way to the Northern, swaying his head this way and that. He sometimes pretended he was a hippopotamus when he was alone. She'd asked him about it one day after they'd snuggled and watched a documentary on cable. That's all they'd done that one blue day: snuggled, watched a show on hippopotamuses and eaten bowl after bowl of popcorn. Her son had brought her so much joy and she never forgot how hot and smooth the back of his neck was, at a week old, even now at eight. She loved to kiss the perfect warmth of his neck and her heart ached when she thought about how the love she knew transformed into everything good when she gave birth to her sons. A love she knew for the very first time. What else did you need in this life, she wondered, but a child who pretended to be a hippopotamus because he thought they dreamed with their eyes open underwater.

The old man was waiting in her backseat and she looked at him directly. "Why are you here?"

"I want to see the town. You will drive me." His lips curled around his teeth and they were a yellow she'd only seen on tusks. He wasn't asking. The bottom row was black, probably from snuff. Probably from grinding them down in his hatred for everything.

She started to shake. "I want you to know," she said. "My son is my life. If you do anything to him..." She pressed her tongue into the sharpest part of her chipped tooth. She didn't care if it drew blood. She wanted him to see this. It wasn't trembling in her. It was outrage. "If you touch him or do anything to us, I will kill you."

The old man looked at her and grinned. It was an ugly grin. His eyes were dead, she noticed. No life and for a second she wondered if he was blind, if all these years the way he'd look through you or at you was a bluff. But he closed his mouth quickly and he said, "Your son looks like his father. He is safe..." and his voice trailed off.

"I will drive you around after we drop off the groceries. I can't have anything else happen to him bad in this life. He's been through enough."

In his heart, he had to know what a son meant to a mother. And then she remembered the coffin at the funeral. It was so small. The boy's father had carried it by himself as the pall bearers walked behind him with their heads bowed. His handsome face down and his shoulders shaking as the tears fell on the pine box.

White shirts now at a funeral, she noticed. No more black suits. White shirts, for hope, she guessed. Life everlasting.

Robby came back to the car and jumped in with a smile. He'd grabbed everything he'd been asked to, plus a ring with a sweet jewel he could suck on. The jewel on the top was as big as a rock and she narrowed his eyes at him. Even in a time like this, he'd sneak something sweet. But she let it go. Today was about getting home safe and clean from medicine.

"Here you go," Robby went to hand the old man his drink. Celestine snatched the can from him, placed herself once again between her son and the old man and handed the elder his drink, careful not to let her fingers touch his.

The old man nodded and she saw his fingernails. They were long, yellow. Filthy.

"*Mahsi,*" he said.

She looked at him and looked at her son and turned her back. She popped her can open and was about to drink when Robby said, "Cheers everybody."

She quickly touched his can to his. She could tell Robby was going to ask the old man for a cheers, too, not to actually cheers the old man but to study him.

"*Wyndah,*" she said quickly. Look.

Robby's bottom lip darted out quickly and he did.

Celestine started the car and looked around before pulling forward. She drove slowly, drove carefully. She wondered if this is what a police officer felt like with a killer in the backseat or the bomb squad felt like with a bomb that could go off anytime in their hands, in their faces.

They made their way home and the old man would sneeze after each sip of his pop. "*Neezee,*" he'd say and Robby started to giggle. He glanced sheepishly at his mother with a grin that he saved only for her when something happened he found funny and wanted to see if she found it funny, too. She didn't smile. She focused on the road and her heart, she realized, was cold with fear.

Richard Van Camp

Celestine could see her whole family standing at the window when she pulled up. Word had travelled. Word had traveled fast that she was driving the devil around.

"Robby, come inside. *Ho!*"

"I'm staying with you," he said.

"*Zunchlei*," she said and gave him the look.

"I'll be right back," she said to the rearview mirror and it was his eyes that gave him away. He was tired, lonely. His face was so foul, dark and bony, with those ancient teeth but his black eyes gave him away. *Who else did he have?*

She made sure to take Robby's can of pop with her, and her own when she made her way to the house. She left nothing he could touch that was hers, but could he plant something? Could he slip something into the fabric of the seat that could hurt them?

"What's going on?" her mother asked.

"How come you're driving him, you?" her eldest brother asked.

"Celestine, what's happening?" her father asked.

She explained that the old man wanted a ride.

Then they'd gone after Robby. "You're staying here. We can't talk sense into your mother. Did he touch you? Did he touch your hair?"

"No," he'd said and walked to his mother's side, no longer sucking on the ring. "I'm going with Mom. I won't stay here." His sticky hand had found his way into hers and the ring stuck to her hand, and she was suddenly strong.

"Tell him," her father said from his chair. "If he wants to be a man today, tell him."

The family grew quiet.

"Robby," she said as she crouched to his level. She swept his bangs out of his eyes. "Robby, this is a dangerous old man. This man has power but he uses it for bad."

Robby nodded. She looked into the eyes that were his father's and her heart warmed with what she needed to say. "You," she said. "You have power. You knew before any of us that Grandpa passed away, remember? Remember how he woke you up to kiss you goodbye?"

She could see the family make the sign of the cross and nod. Her mother leaned against the counter. Her apron was covered in white flour, a jam streak across the front.

"You have always had power, *inkwo*. But you use it for good, right?"

Robby smiled. "I have power?"

"You have power," she said. "So we have to be careful. If you're going to come with me, you have to do exactly what I say, okay? No arguing, no being cheeky, okay?" Robby nodded and went back to sucking his ring. "I promise."

Celestine turned to her family. "Robby promised."

They shook their heads.

"Groceries," she pointed with her lips, a Cree thing, she thought. *I live with the Crees in Smith and it shows.* "We have to go."

"We'll pray," her mother said. "We'll pray for you when you're with him."

She nodded, touched.

"Take this," her mother said. A rosary. Her mother's rosary. The one she was never allowed to touch. It was there. Warm and covered in flour. She placed it over her daughter's neck and she was kissed on both cheeks. Her mother squeezed her hands. "My girl," her mom said. "Be safe."

Celestine took a big breath, ran her tongue over her chipped tooth and glanced at the wall where her wedding photos used to hang. Years after she'd left, the family had kept them up, despite her taking them down. As if to punish her for leaving. Finally, she burned them. It was never talked about. In the place of her wedding photos were the pictures of her two sons who weren't with her: Francis and Jordan. She prayed that one day they'd return. They'd stopped wanting to talk with her on the phone, even on her birthday, even on theirs. Letters, parcels, presents— she'd lost count of how many she'd sent through the mail and she knew, instinctively, that they'd never be delivered by John.

Again, she ran her tongue along her chipped bottom tooth: a reminder of a savage hit when she least expected it one night in the truck on the way home as the boys slept only inches away. She'd bled quietly into her hands, in complete shock. A jealous rage from John after a night of dancing. One chief came up to ask how her father was. Her father had fallen through the ice on his machine and had climbed to safety and walked back to Rae before anyone knew he was in trouble. She'd answered quickly that he was good. But she caught the furious eyes of John watching from the kitchen, his coffee cup mid-chest. The hatred in his eyes. She held snow up to her face, in her mouth, over her eyes as John woke the boys. She'd stood outside for what seemed like hours as he put them to bed and she felt the chip in her tooth and did not want the sun to rise in the morning or ever again. She could not believe this was her life and was suddenly filled with shame. She had become one of the women she swore she never would become with a man she'd loved, had a family with, cooked and cleaned for. Adored.

Robby had always been the one to stay with her. Her other sons had gone with their father during the split. They rarely called and she suspected that John had poisoned them against her with lies. What had the counsellor said? Shame the parent and shame the child?

They made their way to the car and Celestine said quickly, "Remember what I said, Robby," she said. "Exactly what I said."

"Roger that," Robby said. And he used the voice they used when they pretended they were truckers. They did this when he was in the bath and she was preparing his lunch for the next day.

Her voice, she realized, was the voice she'd used the morning she left with him years earlier, after being tied up with a phone cord and beaten with a phone book over and over. She'd waited until John had passed out. He'd hit her so hard that he'd loosened the cord and she'd snuck into the room at the end of the hall. All night she'd whimpered and cried into her shirt so she wouldn't wake Robby to terror. The other two boys, her other two sons, had already been shipped off to his parents', but Robby wouldn't leave. As a baby, he'd never been far from her.

Even when she used to bide her time through a beating, she learned to fall into a punch, a slap, a hit. To roll with it and put a picture of each son between a fist, a kick, a backhand. To bide her time until he passed out, waiting for the sunrise she hoped would never come after a night of hell, but looking forward to the freedom the day brought with his work, his drinking with friends, his mysterious two hour coffees with friends she knew were out of town.

She shuddered when she remembered crawling in her own blood to go get her son that last morning with John. There had been a baby. He never knew. She lost it. She lost it to a punch and a kick. In her dreams, it was a girl. A girl reaching for her. A girl with long black hair and, in her dream, it was her when she was younger.

They got back into the car.

The old man did not ask about her family. He did not pretend to care. They drove.

And she noticed the town already knew. Cars and trucks started to follow her. People stood on the corners waiting for her to cruise by so they could see the devil in the backseat.

Richard Van Camp

The old man began: "Whose place is that?" "Who owns that lot?" "What are they building there?"

Celestine did her best to answer but it was apparent to her that Rae had changed. *Behcho Ko* was no longer her home. She used to know where everyone lived. Now, it was a guessing game. New houses. New lots. A playground left to rot. Children everywhere but no parent watching them.

Robby did his best to answer when she couldn't, and she was surprised with what he knew. She marvelled at what a young man he was becoming, already at eight. So wise. So gifted with everything he tried. She could see how he spoke with his hands, like her mother, and he took his time between thoughts like her father. He'd sit through hours of storytelling, not moving and she could sometimes hear him repeating the stories in the bathtub to himself. And, at night, he'd sometimes sing in his sleep.

"Where do you live now?" the old man asked her.

She glanced in the rearview mirror. "Me?"

The old man nodded.

"Fort Smith. I go to school now."

"Do you miss Rae?"

She thought about it. "It's nice to visit."

She glanced back in the rearview mirror and saw him looking at her ring finger. She'd thrown her wedding ring into the Rapids of the Drowned in Smith summers ago. The old man was quiet.

"Smith is fun," Robby said. "We have pelicans and a little bat that sleeps in the church. He doesn't care who sees him."

The old man listened to Robby speak of Smith. Celestine watched him listen. She suspected he was hunting for something. This question was a lure. Celestine touched Robby's knee. "Okay, so that's Rae. Where would you like to go now?"

"Edzo," the old man said and it was an order. She wondered if he was hunting someone now, gathering information for his next target. She worried she and Robby were being used for evil. But he was not asking. He was looking around and she watched him. She was sure that in his day, he must have been handsome but feared. His clothes were old, dusty. She wondered how long before the earth would have him? How long before he passed and took all he knew with him? She wondered what the moment was when he gave into it all, gave into the dark power of *inkwo*. What did it promise him? If it was wealth, she could not see it; if it was power, he had it, but the cost was no family, no friends, a life walking alone, no children.

Edzo was a ten-minute drive away. The old man was quiet as they drove. It was October. She could see the moon in the sky. Far away. The ancient moon. Full. The quiet majesty of her. What was happening on the land? She used to know these things. The little wolves who were too small would be left behind as the families with the stronger pups taught them to hunt and track. Same with the bison outside of Smith. The calves and the cows would make their way to the winter ranges. But what of the men—the bulls? What would they do? She used to know. She used to. And cranberries. Was it the low bush or high bush that were ripe now? There was frost on her shoes and on Robby's when she walked him to JBT in Smith, and they loved it. The steam from their mouths in the morning and at night. The silver perfection of the frost, the quiet, the wood smoke starting to blanket the town with its sweet smell. Teaching herself to sew. Teaching herself to bake. Reading cookbooks. Eating good. And the peace of a bed where sleep was promised. A safe sleep. A glorious sleep. No waiting out sex she didn't want. No crying or bleeding into a towel. No terror.

She saw the full moon and remembered what she'd always called it each time it was perfectly round: the moon of letting go. She'd always given the worst of her life to the moon. She trusted her with it. She let it go and moved on. She moved on and gave it to her ancestors.

Soon they were in Edzo. The families who lived there were looking out of their windows, standing in their yards, waiting in their idling trucks for them. They knew. They knew the devil was where he never went. They must have sensed he was looking for something, someone. They watched the way she imagined dogs on chains waited for the wolves to come for them. Soon the questions began: "Who lives there?" "Whose land is that?" "What are those kids up to?"

"Swimming," Robby answered.

"Where?" the old man asked.

"In there," Robby said. "The swimming pool."

"Eh," the old man said. "Kids don't swim there."

"Sure they do," Robby said. "They swim in there. It's fun."

The old man looked at Celestine, puzzled. She found herself smiling. She nodded at him and, for a second, for a second they could have been a family: an *ehtse* and his daughter with a grandson cruising on a Sunday. But she caught his eyes and he was looking for something. She knew it. He flashed his eyes at her and she looked away.

"Where's your wife?" Robby asked suddenly, directly to the old man.

"Robby," Celestine snapped.

"No wife," the old man said and raised his hands up simply. *"Dowdee."*

"Robby," Celestine said. "That's not polite."

"Well, where's all his grandkids?" Robby asked and popped the jewel into his mouth.

"Robby," she scolded and glanced back. The old man closed his eyes.

"I'm ready for home," the old man said and she made her way back.

● ○ ●

Medicine

Her kidneys had ached every day for two years after that. She never told anyone, not even her doctor. It was as if her body punished her. She worried John had sent bad medicine her way for leaving but she knew inside it was the grief: the tension leaving her. Her body letting go.

She remembered something no one else would ever believe. When she was younger, her family had traveled to Wekweti. How old was she? Fifteen? There were hand games, a drum dance, the annual Dogrib Assembly. It was there one night that her mom had asked her to walk with her to play cards at an old man's house. That's where the community went. It was there that her mother told her that the man who owned the house wasn't a man at all. He was a bear. Oh her blood turned to gasoline when she heard that and she wanted to run. She wanted to be safe. But her mom told her that he was the last of his kind, the last of the old ways. And that her mom was just as scared but wanted to see him, wanted to shake his hand.

"You see," she explained, "the man could not leave his house for eight months. But he missed the people and the people honoured him. They brought delicacies for him and his wife. Ducks, moose nose, caribou, rabbit brains, blood soup, fish. They fed him and his wife, his poor wife. She cooked for the community and the people visit, talk, sip tea, play cards for matches. No money. No *sombah*. They do it to keep him company because he misses the people, and you will meet him so you see the last of his kind. He was born a bear; he was born a man. He is the last of the old medicine, and he is our relation."

And so she went and walked in with her mother and her mother held her hand as they walked in and the house rose quietly to meet them: hugs, handshakes, people pulling her hair gently with a smile, telling her to let it grow, let it free. Get it nice and long like how her mother used to wear it, and she was young and proud to see everyone and then they nodded towards the kitchen. They looked with pride and respect towards the kitchen. Respect for the man and his wife. The man who was a bear. The man who was the last of everything, the last of the old magic that the earth remembered, and she went with her mom, hiding behind her and she saw him. She saw the man. He was black and big and round. A giant. He rolled his head back and forth and smacked his lips. He was spotted with large freckles the size of tear drops, and she had never seen a Dogrib so black before and his eyes were yellow, yellow as the old man's nails. *Ancient.*

And her mother walked forward carefully, holding her hand out and the man's wife stood to shake it. Celestine watched the man who was a bear and her heart grew cold with fear. To see him so close. He was a giant. His hands were the size of polar bear paws. Huge. He had jowls like a bulldog but his eyes were kind. His eyes. She could still see them because he did not seem to look through them. He breathed through his mouth and his chest heaved but it was his nose. He continually took in the room through his nose, his scenting the room, and the smacking of his lips. He smacked his lips loudly and there was a plate in front of him: a brisket. It had been boiled. The meat was still steaming. The man looked pleased.

Her mother shook his hand and he did not take it. Not like a man. No. He used his paws to cup her mother's hand and, though she heard her mother speak, the man answered in a voice so low she could not make out what he said, and he spoke to her as he smacked his lips. They spoke and Celestine listened. She listened to her mother speak Dogrib, not the kind they use now, but the old kind. The ancient kind. The tongue they must have spoke in Nishi. The kind her grandparents sometimes spoke before they passed. And Celestine was surprised that her mother did not shake, did not tremble.

And then it was her turn. Her mother introduced her and the bear's eyes roamed about her, the ceiling, the wall, but she watched his nose. He was drinking her in through his nose and she watched herself hold her hand out, as if in a trance. He cupped it, and he was gentle. She said hello, *Dante'e,* and he smiled. He was happy to meet her and he told her she would have three sons. He told her Rae would not be her home. He told her to watch the moon. It would tell her everything that was to be, that she was ancient, and she did not know if he meant the moon or her but she was too scared to ask. And she saw the eyes of his wife and she saw a sadness and a duty. A duty to serve the people. She had married the old magic and to do that was to live for the people now, to serve, to honour the people who showed respect to her husband.

Then she was gone. She was back in the crowd. She could not remember how he or she said goodbye. She was pulled into the crowd with hugs, with smiles, with gentle hair pulling, with the embrace of the people. She tried to turn back but there were new guests with fresh ptarmigan. They had brought him plump ptarmigan and snowshoe hare. Soon she and her mother feasted on dry meat, dry fish, fat, pemmican, bannock. The women played cards for matchsticks and the men smoked outside. The man did not like smoke, didn't trust it, he said. It hurt him, the women remarked. That and cats.

Who would believe what she saw? One day she would tell Robby and her sons about the old man, how he took her hand gently. The last of his kind. The last of the old ways. The last of all the earth remembered. And she wondered about his wife. What was it like to live with a man who couldn't leave the house for eight months? What was she without her husband? Who was she without him? Who was any woman without a man? A family? Who was a woman without duty?

"I want you to clean my house for me," the old man said as they pulled into his driveway.

"Momma," Robby said and touched her arm.

She knew. She knew she would. She wanted to. She wanted to see how the old devil lived. She'd keep Robby close but she knew this was the same thing. He was the last of the old world, the old medicine, and she could one day tell her grandchildren about this. This was a gift. A dangerous gift. To earn this story could cost her everything. "I will," she said. "I will if you have the cleaning supplies."

"They left them," he said. "At my door."

"*Mahsi*," he said.

And she could tell he meant it. Something was happening. She knew. She knew she was to do this. If he'd planted something or took something in the car to work medicine, it was already too late.

She knew that this was her chance. Her chance to see how he lived. To be the invited spy. The old man couldn't live forever, she thought. And this is how stories begin. She would wait years to tell someone this and she knew it would be her grandchildren. To kiss the perfect warmth of the back of their necks and nuzzle their ears and to hold the story in, to keep it until they were older, and to share it.

The old man let himself out of the car and made his way to his little room at the old folks home. It was in the satellite building, the farthest one away from the main building and other homes.

"Robby," she said. "We are going to help this man."

"Why?" he asked. He wasn't sucking the ring anymore.

"Because he's asked us to," she said.

"He's bossy," Robby said.

"He is," she said. "And this is why you have to do exactly what I say. You are to stay close to me. *Wyndah*. You are not to step over any of his things: moccasins, moccasin rubbers. Nothing, okay? And you are not to touch anything of his. Not even his cap. Not even his gloves. You stick with me and I'll do the work. You are a boy. One day you will be a man. Today you will see something you will never forget. You will see how a medicine man lives. One day you will tell your family about this. It's good that you learn now. It's good that you do this with me. One day he will be gone but you'll have this memory. You'll say you helped your mom clean an old medicine man's house."

Robby nodded. He looked out the window and nodded again. This was how it started, she thought. How boys turn to men. It's in moments like this and she knew she and only she could do this for the old man. If the old man asked, then he couldn't harm them, could he?

She turned with her son and walked towards the old man's house. He'd lit a small pipe made of red willow and was smoking, looking off towards the sky. She could see the cleaning supplies: a mop, a broom, a dustpan, a two pack of yellow gloves, sponges, Mr. Clean, bleach, rags.

"I keep my medicine in an old wooden box in my bedroom. Stay away from that. Tell your son."

Celestine froze. Ice trickled into her heart. He'd given her something. Where he kept his medicine. She could feel eyes on the back of her neck and turned. Again, curtains closed. The elders were watching. She knew everything she used to clean the house would later be burned.

"*Mahsi*," he nodded but stared straight ahead.

"*Heh eh*," she said and made her way in the house. And it was pitiful how he lived. The smell was of piss, old dry meat, boiled fish, something stale, something rotting. He slept in his living room. There was no couch. There was only an old cot and a radio. There was a calendar from Arny's store from years ago and pictures of the Pope's visit to the north. An eagle fan made of feathers hung on the south side of the room, and it looked old. Once beautiful but old now. Ancient. A moose hide handle. The room was filthy. Dust, dried mud, spider webs.

She opened the pack of yellow cleaning gloves and handed a pair to Robby. "Put these on. *Ho.*"

He started to shake his head.

"Robby," she said and opened the windows. "Stay close. Put these on but don't touch anything, okay? *Wyndah.*"

Robby nodded and put them on. He covered his nose with his hand and she got to work. She started to sweep.

Oh it was pitiful, she thought. To live like this. It was filthy; the place stunk. Most of all, though: there was no life. There were no photo albums, no feelings of a home. This could have been an apartment for strangers. She immediately walked around the house with Mr. Clean and put some in the toilet without looking in, squirted some in the tub without looking, put some in the sink with a little bit of water, put some in a bucket of hot water. She wanted the whole place to smell like lemons. She swept and cleaned and worked fast. She couldn't wait to mop the house and wash the walls. A small place wouldn't take long but she was worried about that trunk in his room.

"Robby," she said again. "No going near that trunk in his room, okay?

"Roger dodger," he said and sat down on the single chair at the man's supper table.

She swept and used the dustpan to collect everything. Strange, she thought. In the dust, she saw three glass beads, all black, and a small earring. Her heart froze. There. In the corner: a finger.

A child's finger. Black. Gnarled. Twisted.

She knelt, made sure Robby couldn't see. Got closer.

No.

A root. *Ratroot?*

She wasn't sure.

She left it.

She didn't know what to do with the beads and the earring, and she didn't want to touch them, so she walked outside and showed them to the old man. *"Na,"* she said. *"Wyndah."*

The old man looked at them and shook his head. *"Dowdee."* He motioned for her to dump it all. She walked to the bushes and dumped everything. She looked up. There was the moon. The beautiful full moon. She could see what seemed to be a wolf sitting on the moon. She studied it and took a big breath. She turned and saw Robby was looking at the old man. The old man said something to him and Robby was smiling. She walked quickly back. "Robby," she said. *"Zunchlei."*

Robby followed her back in.

"Celestine," the old man said and she stopped. "Keep the boy away from that box."

She nodded. She made her way towards her son and ran the water so the old man wouldn't hear them. "What did he say to you?"

"Nothing," he said. But she could tell.

"Robby," she said. "Tell me."

Robby swallowed. "He wanted to know when we were leaving."

"And what did you say?"

"Tomorrow. After breakfast."

Was this bad? Was this bad that he knew?

She shook her head. "Stick close to me. You wanted to stay with me and I let you. Don't speak to him. And do not go into the old chest in his room, okay? Do not even go near it."

"I promise," Robby sighed. He was getting bored. She could see. There was nothing for him to do.

"Go find us some music," she said.

He looked at her.

Celestine pointed with her lips to the little radio and Robby pounced on it. He fiddled with the dials and soon turned on CBC. Norbert Poitras was on: the Trail's End. Straight country.

The kitchen. There were hardly any dishes, so she ran the water and filled the sink with soap to bring a lemon scent throughout the house. She filled it with hot water and began to wipe the counters. Again, she swept and Robby leaned against the counters.

"Are you excited to go back to Smith?"

Robby shrugged.

"What is it?" she asked.

"He's lonesome," Robby said and she paused. He was right. The old man was tired. Lonely. She looked around. What was his life like? What did he think about at night? Who and what haunted his memories? How long could you work black medicine for? How long could you plot? What was promised for a life lived like this? Who did he serve? No kids. No family. No friends. Who?

She cleaned and lost herself in thought. After, the bathroom. Oh it was filthy.

"Wait in the kitchen," she said and gagged. Even though she'd poured Mr. Clean into the sink, toilet and tub, the stench of piss and offal was too much. She turned the fan on and her eyes watered. Oh it was pitiful. Pitiful. She cleaned. She used bleach and a toilet brush, bleach in the tub, bleach in the sink. She cleaned fast and worked hard. Strangely, there were no fingernail clippings or strands of hair anywhere to be found. The medicine man had cleaned his home in his own way for anything of his that could be used against him in a medicine war.

After that, his room. In the middle of the room was a large wooden box. It looked like an old-fashioned grub box, one you'd see in dog sleds. One that was supposed to be filled with pots, pans, grub. It looked beat up. But it sat alone in the middle of the room and she made the sign of the cross and kissed the cross around her neck. She cleaned around it and said Hail Mary over and over. In the closet hung his clothes: two shirts. Two pants. Two pairs of socks. They were all filthy. She threw them in the washer and got to work. In the closet, his parka. No moose hide, no beaded gloves. Pitiful.

But that was it. That was all he had.

She got to work and cleaned and cleaned and cleaned. Robby helped her wipe the walls. They listened to country and, because it was a small place for one person, they were done. She placed the man's clothes in the dryer and put it on a timed dry that she was sure would be perfect.

She was done.

Celestine kept her gloves on in case there was more to do.

"Nehko honti a tsee lah," she announced to the old man.

He looked ahead and she studied his profile. He'd gotten skinny over the years. Not frail. Not yet. But skinny.

"Mahsi," he said and looked to her. "You've always taken care of the people."

She nodded.

"Zunchlei," he said and waved her towards him.

She walked slowly, aware that Robby was behind her. She could hear him taking his gloves off with a snap. He waved her closer. *"Zunchlei."*

Soon she was standing close. His pipe was gone and he stood to face her. Celestine grew shy.

He looked into her eyes. "Someone is trying to kill you."

She backed up, reaching for Robby. "What?"

He nodded. "This was medicine from long time ago."

"Robby," she said over her shoulder. "Go inside and wait. *Ho.*"

"Roger that," Robby said and went into the kitchen where it was clean, where nothing could hurt him, where he could listen to music.

"What are you talking about?" she asked. "This better not be a trick."

"No trick," the man shook his head. "It was a woman who called this for you."

And she knew. Celestine knew who it was. She knew: *Therese.*

It was John's lover. The whole time they were together, Celestine knew a woman loved John. It was an ex who John never quite got over. Celestine liked the competition. In fact, it was the ex who made the hunt for John so exciting. It was a game. Because of her, Celestine became a better wife, mother, lover and friend. Celestine did her best every day for her and her man and her family to show John that he'd chosen well. And on her wedding day, she remembered thinking as she walked into the church, "I've won."

She also remembered the quick fear when the priest asked if there was anyone who wanted to challenge the ceremony. She wondered for a second if Therese was going to come forward and say something and, to her shame, she could see it in John's eyes, too.

Therese was the one who never got over John—at least that is what John said. Celestine learned a year after they were married that it was the other way around. Therese also came from a family from Wekweti who had a lot of medicine and she made Celestine's life miserable. There were late night calls to the house with no one on the other line. There were calls to John's pager in the middle of the night. There was always a reminder that he was a wanted man.

"Go on," she said.

"This medicine couldn't touch you when you were in Smith. The second you came back here...it's been waiting." He then lifted his hand and pointed over the trees facing south. "The woman who set this up hired a pipe man from Alberta. I can see him and his family. He's young. Strong. I can't touch him but I can kill someone he loves if you want."

Celestine heard herself take a huge breath. "What? No. No...."

He nodded. "I can kill her for you if you want."

"No," she said and moved closer to him. "No killing."

He thought about this. "I could—"

When she looked at him, she saw him as weak. This was all he had. This was all he could offer. She was struck with the image of the father earlier this morning carrying the coffin of his son, how his shoulders shook as he wept, the sound that pierced them all as he started to moan as he cried.

She became furious. "You will not kill anyone. No killing. No cursing or killing anyone. Do you hear me?" And she thought about it. She was free. Her lips were quivering but she was free. They were all free now. "She can have him."

"It's too late," he said. "It's too late for that."

Her heart froze. "What?"

"The medicine," he pointed again to the south, "is coming. It's on its way. You leave tomorrow back to Smith. It will come for you then."

She closed her eyes. This was a nightmare. To return home to a funeral and for the threat of open medicine hunting her. Robby, she thought. We have to head home. A new job. A new chapter. She had to be there. She could not be late.

"*Na*," the old man said. "Look." And his voice changed. He reached into his vest pocket and pulled out a necklace made of moose hide with a little pouch at the base. "I made this for you."

She stared at it. It looked ancient as if it had been worn by many people over hundreds of years. The moose hide was stained with what looked like grease, sweat, oil from hands and earth. She could smell it. It smelled strong, ancient. Yarrow?

"This will take the hit for you," he said. "When it comes. Do not look inside the bag or your son will go blind."

Celestine winced at the thought of that kind of power. She was shaking.

He went to put it over her head. Her skin suddenly came to life in fear. She rose her hands to stop it. "Don't touch me," she said.

He looked at her and his eyes softened. "My girl, I am protecting you. Your son is your life. *Na*."

She felt her hands fall gently to her sides and he placed the necklace over her head and around her shoulders. She could hear him praying, chanting. It was soft and beautiful what he sang. It was the same phrase over and over. She felt safe. She could feel her mother's rosary under the medicine bag and she could feel the old man's hands touch both of her shoulders and then the top of her head.

My hair, she thought briefly, and then it was over.

"My girl," he said.

She had a quick flash of the man who was half bear looking into her eyes and saying something so low she couldn't hear but could feel. The man who was a bear had blessed her in the old way.

She opened her eyes. What he'd placed in the pouch at the base of the necklace smelled of yarrow, yes, boiled yarrow, bear grease and something thick and deep: caribou tongue?

"This will take the hit for you. It knows what to do. After it's done, after it comes for you, burn it."

The old man looked at her and nodded, and then he looked past her shoulders and his eyes widened.

Robby!

Celestine turned around to see that Robby standing wearing the old man's moccasins, the old man's moccasin rubbers, his moose hide vest so old the beadwork looked like dull plastic, his gloves and his hat. "I don't understand what all the fuss is, Mom," Robby shrugged. "These clothes feel just like Grandpa's."

"Robby!" Celestine yelled out of fear. The old man had just touched her. She'd trusted him. And now Robby had broken the most sacred promise of not touching a medicine man's things. "Robby, you take them off right now!"

Robby looked at his mom and pointed at the old man. "But you said he had power. I have power, too. I keep waiting to feel something but it's just cheap, boy. *Wah!* I don't feel nothing."

Celestine was furious. Where did he get these clothes from—the trunk? The trunk where the old man kept his medicine? She raced toward her son. She was enraged. When she heard it: laughter.

Laughter from behind her.

Laughter from the old man.

The old man started to cackle.

She stopped and looked at him and the old man started to slap his knees. It was a belly laugh and the old man laughed and laughed and laughed. Robby started laughing, too, and Celestine watched it all. She realized that she was still wearing her yellow cleaning gloves. She watched it all with her mother's rosary around her neck and the old man's medicine pouch on top. She was protected, wasn't she? But soon she found herself laughing along with Robby and the old man. It was relief and release and each round of laughter started a new one and they laughed and laughed and laughed. Celestine thought for a second that if anyone walked in, they would think: "Oh what a lovely family: a grandpa with his daughter and grandson."

She laughed and walked towards her son. She pulled her gloves off and ordered Robby to take off the old man's things properly, with respect. She touched the old man's moose hide vest and looked to him. "I am sorry, Uncle. Forgive my son."

The old man wiped his eyes and shook his head. "Your son is going to be a great leader," he said. "He will bring you three sons and one daughter."

Robby gulped loudly with his throat. "Sick."

Celestine beamed at the thought of this. "*Mahsi*. Robby, let's put this all back for our uncle, okay?"

"Okay," Robby nodded. "Sorry everybody."

Celestine looked at the old man who made his way out to his porch to have another puff on his pipe. He was shaking his head and laughing. "Robby," she said but shook her head as well. "Let's go home."

As Celestine put everything back, she looked around: the place was spotless, his clothes would be dry in minutes. She was happy.

"Am I allowed to shake his hand?" Robby asked.

Celestine thought about it and nodded. "Well, you already wore his clothes. Why not? Show respect and be polite."

She watched Robby approach the old man, the most dangerous man in the north. Robby was growing. He'd filled out this summer but now it was gone. He had longer legs, arms. His skin was getting darker and she was proud of him.

She looked at the old man and thought, "I have seen your life, old man, and it is lonely. I have. I have. I have seen where you keep your medicine. If anything touches my son, I will know where to go and I will know what to do."

Robby made his way outside and held his hand out. "*Mahsi cho*, Uncle."

The old man smiled and put his pipe down. "*Mahsi cho*, nephew." The old man chuckled and pointed at Robby with his free hand. "You will be a great leader for the people. Lots of trouble for your mom. But you will be a great man. Take care of your mom. She is also a great woman."

Celestine blushed at the generosity.

Robby looked to her and smiled. Oh her heart ached. She would never forget this. Robby shook the man's hand and bowed and made his way to the car. He started swaying his head like a hippopotamus as he got in and buckled up.

Celestine held her hand out and the old man stood. *"Mahsi cho,* Celestine. Travel safe. Remember: do not look into this bag. It will take the hit. It knows what to do."

"What do I look for?"

"You will know," he said. "It will show you."

Celestine nodded. *"Mahsi."*

"Are you sure?" the old man asked and his voice went low.

"I am sure," Celestine said. "No killing." She knew what he was talking about.

He nodded. "What about this woman? This one who sent it your way?"

She thought of the beatings she took, the phone book, the telephone cord, holding snow to her face to stop the swelling. "She can have my ex," she said. "They deserve each other."

He nodded. "Travel safe."

She nodded and shook his hand. It was ice cold. She started but shook it once, gently. *"Mahsi."*

Celestine made her way to the car and got in. Buckling up, she looked at her son who was fiddling with the radio dials. She was suddenly tired. "Let's go home," she said. And then she remembered the box. "Robby, did you go near that wooden box in his room?"

"No way," he said. "It was spooky."

She knew he was telling the truth.

"So where did you get his vest and gloves?"

"In his dresser."

"Dresser?" she asked. "I cleaned that whole house. There was no dresser."

Robby began munching on his chips. "Mom, there was a dresser in the room with that chest. That's where his vest was."

Celestine thought about it. She could not remember a dresser. She was puzzled. She shook her head. Perhaps this was a trick the old man had played on her. She did not know. She would think about this later, but, in her heart, she knew there was no dresser.

They drove home and, as they did, Celestine could see people standing on the road, standing on their porches, standing in their yards. They were all watching her and her son. Celestine stared straight ahead and drove home to where supper was waiting: caribou stew and hot bannock with lots of tea and jam. Coffee. Ice cream and apple pie for dessert. The TV was on. How she hated to eat with the TV on. But she was too tired to say anything. After, a hot shower for her, scrubbing herself raw and a bath for Robby. She hugged him and sang to him and he fell asleep like that and she beside him. She woke in the middle of the night to Robby turning over.

She got up, made her way to her room and her father waiting for her. He'd been waiting. He stood and hugged her and told her they'd prayed all day. "Did he touch you?"

"No," she shook her head. "No."

"Your mother was worried," he said.

"I know, Dad."

"Get some sleep, my girl," he said. "You have a long drive. Thank you for coming home."

She nodded and wiped tears from her eyes and undressed in her room, climbed into fresh sheets. A Bible fell on the floor. She'd missed it coming in. She picked it up and placed it on the dresser, showed it respect and slept with a dream.

In it, she stood in the old man's room, at the base of the old chest. A voice told her, "His medicine is not here. It is behind the eagle fan in the living room."

She flashed awake. Whose voice? She wondered. Her father's? Or was it her grandfather's—or Robby's?

She fell asleep after listening to the house, the house she grew up in, her family dreaming together.

Richard Van Camp

● ○ ●

The next morning the family was gone: perhaps to church, perhaps to pray on the land, perhaps to keep away from her. It was her mother's birthday next month so she knew she'd be back, but she had to leave. Her boss was expecting her and this was a new day, a new job starting tomorrow. It would take her ten hours to drive to Smith, and she would take it one second at a time. She saw the packages that had been set aside for her: ham and cheese sandwiches, a large water jug, dry meat, dry fish, pemmican, fat, and an eagle feather to hang off her rearview mirror. The stem had been beaded with Dogrib blues, reds, and a single bead of yellow. Who had made this, she wondered. Her mother?

She got into the car, gassed up, asked the attendant to check her tires, her oil, her washer fluid. She asked Robby what he wanted for a drink and snacks and he said apple juice and barbeque chips.

She let him. How could she say no on a day when it would come for them?

She bought a pouch of Drum tobacco and pulled over on the bridge, across from the Blackduck camp, and dropped tobacco.

"Robby," she said.

Robby got out, rubbed his eyes and took a pinch out.

"Let's pray for a safe journey."

"I pray for my dad and brothers," he said and quickly dropped the tobacco and deftly grabbed some more, "and for my mommy and for every hippopotamus who is dreaming right now."

Her heart ached and he went back into the car.

"For the old man," she said. "For John and for my boys. For my family. For a safe journey. I need to get home. For the man who sent medicine my way and the woman who asked him to. I pray for you."

● ○ ●

Robby started blowing kisses at the full moon and she smiled. She'd taught him to do that when he was a baby and it was something they did together every full moon. She joined him and they started to laugh. "For our aunty the moon," she said. He nodded. "For our aunty the moon." They walked together. She brushed the top of Robby's hair as he made his way to the back. She buckled him in and surrounded him with blankets and sleeping bags and laundry.

He went right to sleep.

She drove and took her time.

● ○ ●

It came for her over the trees. Robby was asleep in the back seat.

She was watching the full moon as it raced alongside her car far away in the trees. She felt the medicine hunt her before she saw it as the medicine bag around her neck heated. And that's when everything slowed.

She saw it as a comet with a tail of yellow fire. It came for the car to get her and Robby. It struck the rear end of the car, blowing out the tire, lifting the car half off the ground with a shock wave.

She looked back and saw Robby sleeping. She lifted her feet off the brakes and gas as the car lifted entirely off the ground and she watched the rubber of the tire blow out across both lanes of the road.

Her instinct would have been to slam on the brake but she knew: she knew that whatever medicine they sent was counting on this. She calmly kept her feet off the gas and steered towards the ditch where the grass had grown wild. Never, she thought. Never would she have done this and time slowed, it slowed, time slowed and when the car landed, it landed with a bounce. She braced for a solid crunch, but the car raced, the car raced and it slowed, it slowed, it slowed, the belly pan of the car swept with the slowing hands of the grass and earth beneath it.

She looked back and saw Robby sleeping and the car was gently cradled in the ditch where it rested.

As if in a dream, Celestine watched herself stand outside the car. She watched herself jack the car, use the tire jack to remove the bolts, roll the spare from the trunk and replace the tire without a word. The whole time Robby slept. The whole time. She replaced the nuts and tightened them, just as John had shown her.

And the whole time she heard herself singing. Perhaps it was the old man's chant. Perhaps it was the man who was a bear's song. Perhaps it was his wife's. It was somebody's song once and now it was hers. Her body hummed with this song and it was a chant. She sang and was comforted. She watched her hands work the same way she watched her hand reach out to the old man's and to the man who was born a bear. The same hands that had raised three boys who were becoming men. The same hands that were free now.

Celestine dropped tobacco and gave thanks for the old man. She gave thanks for his protection. She ran her tongue along her chipped tooth and dropped tobacco for her parents and for the little boy who never woke up and his family. She thought of her ex-husband, his easy smile, his hands. The way he loved his sons with everything he had, the way he used to love her. Her heart ached with the memory of him holding their boys when they were babies. She closed her eyes and whispered, "I give you back." She got back into the car, watched Robby sleep and drove the car slowly back onto the road and kept driving.

One day Robby will be a man, she thought. One day he will look back and I will tell him this story. One day....

She kept driving, watching the patient moon, and never, not once, did she look back.

TEACHINGS

I Count Myself Among Them

My supper had just been put on the table when two Indians rolled into Yang's. I was in the community we call Outpost 1, British Columbia. It was Easter. I was the only customer there. The men looked rough: dark, dusty clothes, scuffed cowboy boots. They wore hoodies and had them up and over their heads with large sunglasses on. Short hair, though, from what I could see. A lot of the Indians I seen around town had long hair. I'd say they were in their early thirties. One was slim and the other was heavy, had maybe thirty pounds on me. Slim cradled his right arm in a fresh cast and had a bruise across both eyes, as if he'd been struck with a two-by-four. Both had tough faces and stared right through me, which was refreshing as my height usually brings out the Carnival Effect in everyone: astonishment, awe, suspicion. I'm quite fair and often invisible to other Indians when I'm out of the NWT. Sometimes, a lot of times, this can bum me out, but not tonight. I wanted to eat my meal and make the drop at nine o'clock. I had an objective. The brothers sat down behind me and started bossing Yang around: "Hey, how you're doing? Remember us? How's that iced coffee?"

A bear—or something like one—started growling outside the window. I jumped. *What the hell was that?*

Heavy started yelling at Yang: "You got fresh iced coffee?"

Yang said nothing. He only looked down. When I went to the bathroom to wash up I couldn't help but notice a baseball bat under the cash register sitting ready for business.

"Chumps!" Slim called out. "It's okay now. Go find some shade."

"He'll be fine," Heavy said. "He's not a pup anymore."

"Never mind," Slim fired back. "He's my nephew."

Nephew? I don't get it. There was some whimpering from outside the window and the men started speaking quietly behind me. *Shit, why did I have to sit here?* Reuben would be mad if he knew I'd let myself get into this position. Not that I had enemies, but I had orders from the Coalition. This was my first trip where they weren't checking up on me every half hour, so I had to prove that I could be trusted. Pistol had a cluster migraine, a "suicide headache" as he called it, and Reuben was delivering his haul to Prince George. Ever since the Night Crawlers mailed Pistol a picture of his wife and kids he'd become a child and started getting suicide headaches. Reuben and I didn't have families so we were left to continue our business. I started to eat my chicken hot pot quickly in case things got ugly. These boys were trouble and Yang knew it.

"We want iced coffee!" they said again. "Iced coffee!"

"Okay," Yang said calmly, as if he'd heard this a hundred times before. "I get it for you. Iced coffee to go, okay?"

I started sipping my Ginger Ale—Indian Champagne, I call it—but it was ice cold so I kept sneezing when I hurried. I was worried the boys would start into me, call me white and want to start something. I had to get to my meeting at nine and I could not be late. I had three kilos of cocaine in my trunk that I was to deliver to my contact here in Outpost 1. I had an address, a time, but I was two hours early. I pride myself in my work and this was my first time here.

Yes, ever since I became acquainted with the Syndicate life has been sweet. All my life I felt like I was living backwards, when all I ever wanted was to belong to something. Like for the first thirty years of my life I was in a daze. I never knew where I was going, as if I was on a hunt but I didn't know what I was hunting. This led me to jail several times but I feel as though, at thirty-four, my life now has a plan before me. If it wasn't for jail, I'd never have met Ghost Bear, our elder in residence. I used to be a mean dog that didn't belong to anyone, but things are getting better for me. People don't call me Flinch anymore. Not since I joined the Syndicate. It's like Reuben, Ghost Bear and Pistol believe in me, and when I have that I am unstoppable.

Because of Ghost Bear, I now eat better. Also, I was too big to fit in the sweat so he asked me to be a doorman. How's that for a positive? The Syndicate has also given me direction and purpose and I deliver, and all it took was stepping up when I saw what was coming. That was when Pistol and Reuben were in the sweat. The wardens had welded a bar across the points of the pitchfork I was using to bring the grandfather rocks with, so it could not be used as a weapon, and the spades had been shortened and blunted. I was the doorman for the sweat lodge and spotted two members of the Night Crawlers coming through the sage, squash, corn and beans other inmates had planted. As a doorman you protect those in the sweat lodge you are responsible for. When I saw the shanks I tackled both men before the guards came. I kept squeezing my hands up and down the arms and legs of the attackers, enjoying the pop and crunch of bone beneath me. It was like those long tubes of lights in cafeterias. The bone that shot through one of the men's arms looked like a tooth.

There was no blood. There was no blood. Ever since then, Reuben and Pistol have been using me as muscle and I let them. But, you see, we are stopping people worse than us from coming to BC. There have been executions, torture, a mother shot to death in front of her four-year-old child—all organized by the man I'm to meet tonight.

Ghost Bear's teachings have never left me. I am walking the Red Road. He told me once about contraries: those who live their lives backwards, "Like those who laugh at funerals and those who cry at weddings," he said.

"That's me," my breath caught with emotion. "That's what it feels like to be me." I wondered if I was one and he shook his head. "You are a child of something else, and everything is leading you to something," he said. And that's all he said to me about that.

What was funny was when I was driving into Outpost 1 I saw what looked like an angel engraved into the sides of the mountaintop. It was huge and made out of the snow that hadn't melted yet from winter. Its wings were spread for what must have been miles up there through the beetle-kill and you could even see a tail with its head looking east. How I wish Ghost Bear was there with me. We could have prayed and dropped tobacco and he could sing a song to blanket me and I him. The best part of my incarceration was learning new songs and holy ways.

"I want Salisbury steak," Heavy said.

"Make that two—to go," Slim added, slapping his good hand down hard onto the table. "I'm paying."

Yang nodded and went in the kitchen and stayed there.

The two men started whispering and then they raised their voices. "I don't do that," Heavy said. "You know I don't do that. How many times I told you...."

"No, no," Slim said. "Just keep it down."

"I'm in charge of taking care of you and I say *No,*" Heavy said.

They started whispering again and Chumps started growling outside the window. He sounded huge.

Shit sakes, my hot pot was really frickin' hot and I could tell that both men were getting edgier. Yang came back with two Cokes.

"Is this iced coffee?" they asked.

"No more ice coffee. Have Cokes."

The men were silent.

Yang went to the window and looked for a long time. You could tell he was keeping one eye on the room 'cause it was tense. I knew exactly what would happen if Reuben and Pistol were here. Reuben would stand and block the door while Pistol turned around and told them to settle the fuck down before demanding to be compensated for being disturbed. But I couldn't do that. I'm what you would call a gentle giant.

The men were quiet until I heard them crack their Coke cans open and they started to drink. I wondered what Yang was thinking about. Country was playing on the radio. I couldn't make out the artist but it sounded pretty good. "God Bless the Broken Road" was the song. I think that's what it was called. I tried making out the words. It was a stirring song, one that appealed to the patient hunter inside of me.

The men started whispering again. "No, no, no," Heavy said. "I won't do it. You can't make me. Aunty said you're not the boss of me."

"Settle down," Slim said. "Shhhhhh."

I could feel them both turn around and look at me. Chumps started to growl again. Shit that dog sounded huge. If I had to leave in a hurry, he'd be waiting for me outside and I'd have to get through him to the trunk. I wouldn't like to hurt a dog. Their bones feel like they belong in horses. When I gave my report, I'd have to leave this part of my journey out of it, as I was cornered. Pistol would never let that happen to him. Never.

I did my best to eat my meal but was wondering what they were talking about. Maybe they knew about the angel on the mountaintop and what it meant to the people of Outpost 1, so I listened. Pistol told me that Rule Number One as a Road Man is to "shut up and listen 'cause that's how you learn." You learn to sense the undercovers, the snitches and the players who play the killing role in things.

But you also find people on the Red Road from all races. How I love to talk with them and learn. I learned from someone in Mission that a bear always knows what you are thinking. I learned from a lady on Salt Spring Island that dragonflies are the revivers of snakes and can sew the lips shut of any child who's just told their first lie. I even learned from a carver in Gibsons, that place where they filmed *The Beachcombers*, that butterflies are guardians for lost souls.

I always try to learn something about the land I've traveled through and the people I've met here in BC, and it seems to me that BC needs a good fire to take care of these pine beetles because they have eaten, from what I've seen, half the province's trees. You can see the rust of where they've been carpeting the mountains and valleys. But I am always trying to learn. This way when I find my next wife and settle down, I can be the man who points out things to my family as we drive on by. I'm not going to be with Reuben and Pistol forever. I have plans: start a family, settle down, spend the second part of my life over with the innocence that jail or past hunts can't touch.

Chumps started up again, growling at something. This time it sounded like he was really angry, getting ready to charge.

"No tail," Yang said to him outside the window. "You big but no tail." I caught him glance at where the register and bat were.

"He's half wolf," Slim said. "Likes to fight."

Half wolf? I wondered. Everybody I know who had a big dog said they were half wolf, but this time maybe Slim was right. I'd love to see Chumps.

"How come he bit you?" Heavy asked. "I told you to shoot him."

"Never mind!" Slim said. "I'll shoot you!"

Oh great, I thought. *Chumps was an attack dog.* I could not miss my meeting. What the hell was I going to do? Good thing the cell was in the car. If Pistol called and asked for a report he would not be happy with how this drop was going. And then he'd put Reuben on the phone and I'd really get it.

"Hey," Heavy called. I turned. They were looking at me. "You're Indian or what?" he asked.

I nodded. "I am."

"Holy shit," they looked at each other. "Aunty said we'd meet a brother today."

I smiled. "I'm from the north. Dogrib."

"Dogrib no less," Slim smiled. "You're wolf clan?"

I nodded that I was. "Are you on the Red Road?" I asked.

They looked at each other and grinned. "Aunty spoke and she was right," Slim said.

"We answer to her," the other nodded and they both smiled.

"Are you on the Red Road?" I asked again.

"Brother," Slim said. "We *are* the Red Road."

I liked this. This felt good to my spirit. Now was my chance. "Do you know about that angel," I asked. "On the mountain?"

They looked at each other and nodded. "She said you'd ask about that too and that would be the sign."

"Sign," I said curiously. "For what?"

"To tell you the story," Slim said.

"Indian way, uh?" Heavy said and nodded.

"Tell you what," Slim offered as his hard eyes softened. They rose together and Slim pulled out a crumpled up twenty, tossing it on the table. "Want to see a miracle?"

I nodded and rose. Both boys stopped and their mouths dropped when they saw the full size of me. People think I'm a big dumb Indian but I'm not at all. I used to measure how tall I was but now I measure it in the shock of those around me. Yang came out with their orders. He'd put their food in Styrofoam containers so they'd have to leave or in hopes that they'd leave. Slim held up his hand. "Uncle, got any plastic bags?"

Yang nodded and gave a look of relief that Heavy and Slim were leaving. He turned around and walked back into the kitchen. He glanced at me and gave me a look that said *this happens all the time.*

"What's the name of that mountain with the angel?" I asked.

"Cheam Mountain," Slim said.

The men walked towards me. "That's right," Slim smiled. He was actually quite handsome. "We'll show you."

Yang came back out, and this time the containers were in two plastic bags. "Here's your supper," he nodded and handed Heavy two doggy bags. Oh that Salisbury steak smelled good.

I looked at Yang and he and his cook stood in the doorway to the kitchen. I knew the cook wanted to get another good look at me. *Shit!* I had almost forgotten to pay my bill. I reached into my pocket and pulled out my wallet. The men looked away as I flipped it out. I had three twenties and left one on the table. "Keep it," I said, at which Yang gave me an uncertain smile, nodding quickly, "Thank you. Thank you. Yuh. Yuh. Yuh."

I glanced at the clock. I had an hour and forty-five minutes before the drop. This wouldn't take long, I hoped. I made sure to walk behind both men in case things came to blows. I had to duck to get through the door. We walked out and where there was once a pitter-patter of smaller clouds they were now gathered in darkness. I rose to my full height again and stretched before flanking them. This was their territory and I was a guest, but I was also a trespasser who'd now deviated from my objective. I would be respectful but wary. If this was a trap I would kill the dog first before baptizing both of them and any others among them. The sky was gathering for something. Maybe rain was coming soon ... or lightning?

There stood Chumps, a black dog of mixed breed. He was a medium sized dog: half wolf, maybe—you could see it in the snout—and his hair puffed out in all directions. Heavy and Slim laughed and walked with their suppers-to-go. Chumps had two little cinnamon dots above his eyes and a Chipewyan woman I knew once told me those were spirit eyes. Those dogs could see the spirit world more clearly than the others. Chumps came up to me and I held out my hand. He sniffed it once and raced ahead to catch up with the men. He ran circles around them as both men laughed.

I was nervous of thunder and, worse, of lighting. Lightning hunts my family to kill us. It killed seven of my ancestors. And that was one thing I hated about BC—the only thing really: storms of lightning, storms with reach. I glanced at my car sitting in the shade. It was armed with a disabler, an alarm, and a club. Pistol's Taser and twelve gauge were in the trunk, but I just wanted to go, to be led to a miracle, by a holy way. The package was safe. It wasn't going anywhere. I was sure I'd be fine, but where had this storm come from? I'd checked the forecast before leaving and it was supposed to be sunny and hot the whole weekend, and now I was being led to something—a miracle they said.

"We'll take you up to the house," Heavy said. "You can meet her there."

"The light will hit in half an hour and her spirit will glow for you," Slim added, pointing at the mountain. "You can meet Aunty."

"You okay?" Slim asked, looking back at me.

I nodded but my eyes gave me away. I felt the air with my hands and I could feel it start to thicken with moisture as a warm wind picked up. *Shit.* A storm *was* coming. Maybe this campaign wasn't a good idea. But the angel on the mountain was starting to glow pink against the darker clouds that filled the sky.

"Sometimes she turns to fire," Heavy said. I looked at the angel in astonishment. Aunty or the angel? I wondered. Who turns to fire? Everything is leading me to something, and I suddenly wanted to be them. I don't know. It seemed that they had something I'd never felt before—a quiet peace.

"Excuse me for asking," I said, "but what kind of Indians are you?"

"We are the not-even-counted," Slim said and looked away. He sounded sad.

"Did you ever hear that story in the Bible about Balaam and the angel?" Heavy asked.

I shook my head. Each time I tried reading the Bible it was only second-hand words of a man-religion, and men were victims of their own compulsions. It wasn't my way. And I ended up not believing any of it. I always thought that God was a white fox watching the sunrise with you every day and to speak to him was to speak to a friend.

Slim cradled his arm and spoke: "There was this old man named Balaam, and he and his donkey were going towards a city, when all of a sudden the donkey locked up and wouldn't move. Balaam had all of his goods with him, like to sell? So he started yelling at his donkey to get a move on. He had to make the market or his family would starve. He had to sell everything on the donkey to make money, and he had to do it fast because he was already late. But the donkey didn't move. It just stared straight ahead. Balaam had quite a temper on him so he pulled out his whip and started wailing on his donkey. Well, the donkey took it—all of it. 'Come on!' Balaam kept yelling, 'Don't do this to me! We've got to make that market!' The donkey stayed still and Balaam went to go hit him again when someone grabbed his wrist. It was an angel. And behind him was an army of angels looking west. 'We are destroying the cities,' the angel told him. 'Had you taken one more step, we would have destroyed you.' The angels looked west. 'Go home,' the angel ordered and the angels moved on in the thousands. Those cities they destroyed were Sodom and Gomorrah."

Both men looked down for a bit and we kept walking. I remember this story. The donkey had spoken the words of God to the man. I remember this but I have forgotten those words. Ghost Bear had once told me that west was the direction of death, and I wished I knew more about this. I had recently gone to Denman Island to find two foot-soldiers of the Night Crawlers. This was retribution for the executions here of two young brothers in the lower mainland. You see, the NCs were moving into BC and allies of ours—the Coalition—had hired us to let it be known they were not welcome. What happened was I found both men and threw one through a wall after punching the bigger of the two so hard his ribs caved.

"Look," I said after I tied them up. I showed them the water-proof box I'd rigged up and said, "This is the box I am supposed to mail your hands, feet and braids in to your boss." They were weeping as I showed them the label with their boss's address. I then showed them my axe and let out a long, tired sigh. "I can either do this or you can leave BC. You're bad people. What's worse is you are Indians. Your mothers never raised you for this. Leave now and I'll let you go. If I ever see you again three of the people you love the most will be mutilated in front of you and it will take days. Days and days and days," I said. "Don't let me do what they can order me to. Please don't. I'm a doorman. I'm a good person. But I'm also an attack dog. We are all soldiers in the wrong war." I tapped where my heart was twice before holding my hands above my head, grizzly style. "Don't unleash me upon you."

They promised to leave, begged to leave, swore on the Bible and on their children that they would never, ever come back to BC again. After, we sat and smudged. The one whose chest caved had pink guck coming out of his mouth, so we fanned the smoke over him. The one who could still speak promised me through the smoke of the sweet grass that they were out, that they would quit this life forever, so I left them like that in their room.

To wash the blood and smoke off, I'd gone for a swim in the ocean alone to baptize myself clean. When I dove in, the water caught fire around me in a holy light. It was phosphorescence. I never knew about it. No one told me. Even with my eyes closed I could see the water ignite around me. The fish I scared bolted, leaving trails of light behind them. Even though the ocean was freezing, I felt like God looking down on Baghdad with thousands of tracers firing below the sky. It was the closest I'd ever gotten to a quiet lightning or feeling like this was where I belonged, and the mighty weight of me knew grace.

The funny thing about the phosphorescence was when I talked about it to the ferry worker, he said he'd gone swimming the night before and watched a sea lion chase fish for an hour in the water, and it was like a comet roaming the earth. Oh I wish I could've seen that. How I wish I could tell my children I saw that. How I wish Ghost Bear was with me. I would have loved to see his talon-pierced chest and the trails of light his braids would have left behind.

The storm was hours away, I was sure, but it wasn't helping my mood. The wicked wicked man I was to meet would call Pistol as soon as we met to confirm the exchange. I looked at my watch. "I have a meeting at 8:30," I said. "I can't be late."

"Don't you want to hear the story of the angel you asked about?" Slim said.

I wanted to learn this story for my family, perhaps the daughter I see in my dreams sometimes. "I do."

"Then who better to ask than Aunty?" Slim asked.

"I do know," Heavy said, "that when the snow of the angel's wings melt it will be the beginning of the end times. The snow in the wings was low in the sixties and that brought a flood they still talk about today. Every time her wings have been low, tragedy has struck this valley. Families were swept away."

I looked at the snow: there was miles and miles of it, but how deep, I wondered. In Penticton, the Okanagans believe that when the snakes come down and speak to the people, that's it—the world is over. The white raven already flew to the people of Haida Gwaii and now Langley; the Crees believe those who see the white raven will be shown that the Big Wind is on its way. Those were the same ones to tell me to never wear red in the summer or I would call lightning to me, so this is why I wear black, black and black.

"Come on," Slim urged. "We're having a feast. Aunty'll tell you."

The only ancestor I had who survived a lighting strike was my great-grandfather and they say that was when he became a medicine man. He lived four years to the day after being hit and what he did during that time was terrifying. Lightning created him. They said he could talk with the animals, mend spirits and bones. They even said he could almost bring the dead back to life. *Almost.*

The grass to my left started to sway with the breeze and the sky continued to darken. I hope wherever we were going was insulated. Lightning can arc and kill you through your plug-ins or windows. It just about got me four summers ago.

We walked down the railroad tracks and made our way towards an older-looking house. There was a sandbox in the front yard filled with toys and a gorgeous Indian woman sitting on the steps having a smoke. She wore a black dress and sat barefoot. Oh her hair was nice and long and her features were sharp and fine. She looked fierce. Her hands and feet were delicate, unpainted. I needed to see her smile. I had to.

There was a bonfire in the distance. Three Indians and a boy stood facing it. One turned our way and nodded. His hair was long, jet black, free. He touched his wrist twice and raised the back of his hand to his forehead. This was a signal to me but I did not understand. Was he deaf or a mute? He nodded to the two men beside him and they approached. The brown boy who walked towards me only had jeans on. His little brown belly looked so cute and his eyes sparkled with a light of their own. He whispered something to the older man who took his hand. The child waved excitedly at me, like he knew me already. I smiled and waved back. What a handsome boy, I thought. The Indian who passed by glanced up to me and nodded. There was something wrong with his right eye. It looked like it was made of glass and was smaller than the other. I returned a nod and smiled at the child. As the boy passed he watched me for as long as he could before the Indian beside him scooped him up to sit on his shoulders in one go. The boy waved with both hands and grinned, blowing me kiss after kiss with a smile.

There I stood, hand mid-air, completely humbled by his beauty.

Chumps stopped and listened for something beside me. The woman's face hardened as she spoke to my hosts. "You're late."

Heavy held out the goody bag and said, "Brought you some hot food, Sister." She appraised me, not surprised or fascinated by my height. Her eyes, her features and her voice softened as I moved close. It was like she'd been waiting to meet me, somehow. "They're praying downstairs," she said to the men.

Richard Van Camp

The men walked ahead and I followed, eager to meet Aunty. As I walked by the gorgeous Indian woman, I smiled. She looked at me and gave me a nod. Her face sparkled with freckles like cinnamon, and her nipples betrayed her. They hardened as I passed by. "Hi," she said. I saw her eyes brighten, like she was relieved to know I was here now, to protect her, to learn from her. "Hey," I nodded, playing 'er cool. I had to see her smile. I just had to. She was traditional. I could tell. There was a dignity to her, a way of knowing that I wanted to learn more about. And I would. I would give myself to her after I met this Aunty and learned more about this people's holy way. Her hands were so dark. Her beautiful skin. She had three hair ties with her, wrapped around her wrist: one red, one blue, one green.

I followed the men into the house and ducked under the door frame before a waft of hot dogs and corn cooking in the kitchen made me hungry again. A large TV dominated the front room; cartoons were on and the kids were laughing. Mattresses had been pulled out as couches for six kids. Paper plates littered the place, filled with half-finished hot dogs and potato chips scattered on the carpet. The boys were watching TV and didn't look to see who we were. Two beautiful girls turned to look at me and they started waving, like they were happy to see me. I smiled, waved back. The girls were adorable. Perhaps when we were done here I could speak with them, make them giggle. Oh my arms suddenly ached to hug them.

Slim stopped and pointed to two of them. "Beautiful, hey?" he beamed and winked. "Twins."

"Really?" I nodded. I did not want to leave them. Oh they stole my heart!

There was a poster of an old Indian standing in a bearskin looking at us as well as a Canadian flag tacked upside down on the wall. There was a huge aquarium in the hallway to my left and the lights were on. The aquarium was filled with hundreds of little lobsters. "Crayfish?" I asked.

"We're having a feast after," the lady said behind me, and she gently touched the small of my back to guide me forward.

We walked into the kitchen and corn bubbled in a giant pot. A few bloated hot dogs sat in the wiener water on the stove. A fresh pot of coffee was brewing. That's what I needed. I'd have a cup after meeting Aunty and make my way to the meeting, before doubling back later to ask this woman for a date. It would be fun to kiss every little freckle she had good night and good morning. Ho Ho!

Heavy and Slim put their doggy bags on the counter and invited me to follow them into the basement of the house. I hesitated but when I heard singing I just had to see what was going on.

That's when I heard the drum. In the basement. "Oooooo," a man's voice sang before again striking a hollow boom out with a drum—deerskin it sounded like. People were singing Indian songs in the basement. My skin rippled with excitement. What I was about to see I could tell my kids one day. I just knew it.

Heavy and Slim made their way into the basement. The woman was right behind me. I ducked as I made my way down the stairs and a smell hit me: wet rust? Sage? Something heavy and human. And what I saw next was beyond belief.

Thirty Indians at least, young and old, woman, man and child, stood around an old steel bed in the middle of a huge room. They were praying for an elder. All the Indians were holding long reeds of some kind in front of them, in front of their faces, the same way one who leads a funeral procession carries a cross. Their eyes were closed and it looked like ash had been smeared across the elder's face. The women wore long skirts, the men deer hide vests and dark pants. Two elders twirled long stalks of a plant I'd never seen before, smoking the room with a thick smell—buffalo sage? Burnt sweet grass?

Something felt wrong with this. They called themselves the not-even-counted and something felt wrong with all of this. "Oh." I stopped.

Richard Van Camp

The woman put her hand gently at the small of my back and motioned for me to continue, so I did. Heavy and Slim made their way to the circle around the elder's bed and I joined them. The people around the elder kept their heads bowed and were all singing a song that went, "Oooo Ooo Oh Oh Ooooo" over and over. A huge man with a drum looked at us and nodded to me before closing his eyes and bringing his drum up into the air and hitting it with a padded drumstick that had everyone singing again. The design on the drum was a black wolf looking up with light shooting out of its mouth and eyes.

Heavy and Slim started singing along. They had taken their glasses and hoodies off and stood like little boys with the crowd. Slim pulled his cast and sling off, and his arm looked fine. Had this been a trick to fool me?

I snuck a peak at the elder in the room and she did not look good: she was just bones and her skin was yellow. Someone had combed her whispery hair out and it was as long as her legs. Around the bed were hundreds of tobacco ties all wrapped in red, black, yellow and green. And there was a blanket of reeds braided like sweet grass to make an altar under her and what was on her face was not ash at all, but a tattoo. I made sure no one could see me and I studied it. Her face was covered with a huge tattoo of a dragonfly, as if it had landed on her face and was laying eggs in her mouth.

"Holy," I said. *What society and ceremony is this?*

The woman nudged me and made a motion for me to bow my head. It took me a few lines to learn the song but I caught on and sang, too: "Ooo ooooo oh oh ooooooo."

At that, the drummer stopped and pointed his drumstick in my direction. I looked around. It was for me. He smiled and invited me forward. Heavy and Slim smiled back at me and motioned for me to follow. I did. I was a bit worried as I did not know the protocol here, but I was calmed, filled with a peace I have only known twice: that swim in the ocean and when I was a doorman and I knew everyone was safe inside the sweat.

I walked ahead and I smiled at all the people I passed, and they all nodded, tipping the reeds they held out towards me. Every single one. I was royalty, an honoured guest. How I wished Ghost Bear was with me, to share this, to see how my life was leading me to good places and good people. He told me that the doorman was the most honoured of all in a sweat, that because I was a protector the spirits honoured me more than anyone. I approached the drummer, cursing myself that I did not bring any gifts to honour the hosts.

"A ho!" he said. "Welcome."

Heavy and Slim nodded and held their hands out and up as if giving thanks for my arrival. I nodded.

"Stand here," the woman whispered and stood beside me. I felt her long thick hair sweep against my arm and was immediately dizzy with her woman power. Our kisses will create a home as I stab her with pleasure. She will understand that I killed bad men for a reason, that I squeezed them until their kicks became little and their mouths opened like children at peace. She will understand me as a child of something else. She will understand me and all the wickedness I put to sleep.

I looked at our elder and her eyes were rolled back and her toothless mouth was open as if in a death mask. Her skin was a sick yellow and my legs began to ache. She was dying.

The drummer pulled a long bone from under his drum. He held it high and looked to the ceiling before handing it to Heavy. Heavy took it and did the same. Slim approached the elder and gently pulled her sweater up. The elder's stomach was so bloated her belly button popped out like a black thumb. She wasn't pregnant. Whatever she had had completely engorged her stomach cavity. It was thick and lumpy, like something small and evil kneeling inside of her getting ready to jump out.

The elder heaved, as if the mere brush of fabric against her skin was agony. She looked left and right. Her yellow eyes started to flutter and she began breathing hard, like a dog without a voice box: *"Hach hach hach."*

"Haaaaaaaaaaaaacccccccccccccccccccccccccccch," she exhaled. Her eyes rolled back and forth in her skull, like they couldn't get a lock on anything in front of her. I winced and instinctively backed up. The smell that rolled off her was dank and wrong for a human. This was the hot smell of death.

The drummer raised his drumstick and brought it down hard once. *Boom!* It rang and I winced. Heavy raised the bone up again and this time I knew what it was: an eagle whistle. I'd seen one in lock up. But it had been sharpened like a shank.

The drummer raised his drumstick again as Heavy raised the whistle like a knife, gripping it like a dagger. "What?" I heard myself say.

The drummer brought his drumstick down onto his angel drum—*Boom!*—as Heavy punched the whistle into the elder's stomach and we heard a huge "Whoomp!" like a blown tire.

"No!" I yelled.

I heard hissing. At first I thought it came from the old woman, but it sounded like it was coming from under the bed, as if something was alive under there. Then I realized it was emanating from someone standing behind me. The people, including the long-haired beauty who'd guided me here, had their heads bowed. They were shaking their reeds to create a wind and they were all humming now. I saw the shirtless boy who had blown me kisses sitting at the top of the stairs. He looked to me and grinned. He held up his hand as if to wave and I saw he had a large feather. I felt immediately weak and wanted to run, but I looked back to see what was hissing behind me now.

Slim walked forward as Heavy stepped back and something black started to bubble out of the top of the whistle. At first it was dark bubbles, but then it spurted, up into the air, on the sheets—like lumpy oil—and that's when Slim moved quickly and put his mouth over it, sucking with all he had, using the whistle as a big straw, to catch what Aunty had coming out of her.

"No," I said and tried to move.

"Watch," the woman said. Her hand pushed against my back.

"This is bad," I panicked.

And that's when Slim raised the eagle whistle towards me, slick with blood, and sprayed it in my face. "Fuck!" I yelled and fell back, tripping. The sick blood was hot, rancid and slick.

As I opened my mouth to yell, he sprayed me again and I gagged, swallowing the blood spew as I tried to breathe and that was when it twisted deeper inside me, popping my rib cage. My eyes were immediately sealed shut by something hot and sticky. I couldn't speak. What I had under my tongue was now in my throat. I couldn't even gag. It thickened and moved like a hot muscled tongue working its way to my stomach. *Ghost Bear,* I wanted to yell. *Help me!*

Hands went through my pockets grabbing my keys and wallet. "Stop," I wanted to say, but nothing came. I tried swinging and kicking but my body was locked as if in seizure. I felt a hundred hands around me, lifting me, kissing my stomach and feeling my hair. "Thank you," they said. "Thank you. You are the way. You are the way." I felt soft reeds grace my body like sharp feathers. I felt myself being lifted up the stairs, through the kitchen and into the living room. I tried smelling the hotdogs and corn and only one nostril worked but all I smelled was a sweet rotting, and it was coming from me. All the while the people sang, "Hooooooooo Hoooooooo Ho Ho Hooooooooooooooo."

They carried me outside. Again I tried kicking, hitting and biting but my body was not my own anymore. My muscles and size were useless. Soon I felt the heat of the bonfire and could hear the wood popping and the rush of fire snapping upon itself, eating the air around it, breathing with tongues of light and lashing.

I was laid to rest on grass. I could feel that much and I felt as if a hundred people were around me. I could hear the wind pick up and branches in the trees started to snap. Thunder started to rumble across the sky.

"Husband," a voice said.

I tried to look around but I was blind. What had sprayed me had hardened inside me. I was frozen.

"Husband," the voice said. "I am here."

"Help me," I tried to say. "Lightning. I can't—"

"You are the way," another voice whispered.

"Husband, I am going to wash you," the woman said. I could hear Chumps panting beside me, like he was thirsty and excited. I felt his hot breath against my hair and he licked my ear.

"I have to go," I tried. "I can't be outside—"

She said nothing. Instead, I felt a hot washcloth spread across my eyes and nose. I was filled with the smell of mint and rust. It took all my strength but I opened one eye to see her looking down on me. She was smiling with tears in her eyes. She was beautiful as she wept and her tears were tears of happiness. She wiped my face gently one more time and what was on the cloth was bloody and black.

"She comes," she said. "Look."

She positioned my head in such a way that I could see the house and the angel on the mountain. My body was filled with something brutal: something completely inside me, and it was bubbling, growing, reaching. I felt sick, felt like throwing up. My stomach started to roll.

The old woman was now a woman in her twenties walking towards us, in a red star blanket carrying the drum. How I knew it was her was because she had the dragonfly tattoo across her face. Her hair was longer, sweeping behind her, and she looked at me with a peace and grace and command. I felt my body growing cold with every step she took.

I looked up to my left. Heavy and Slim now had the faces of otters. They looked at me and nodded. "You're a wolf who's been limping your whole life," one said. The other nodded. "The smell of humans has kept you weak."

Even though they had otter faces, their hands were human. The firelight flickered off the black orbits of their eyes. Three figures approached me from the shadows of the bonfire and they were men who had otter faces, too. They looked at me and tilted their heads left. One looked to Slim and handed him the three bags of cocaine.

"Wait," I tried but my voice started to leave me. What was inside me was now pushing up, trying to stand, causing me to arch my back, pushing my heels against the earth.

"Hey!" I said and tried to raise my arm.

Something started to bubble in my stomach. Cancer? Was it cancer tumoring inside of me? I felt it push my lungs and voice box up towards my throat. One otter handed the black leg bone to the other and he started to slice each bag of cocaine open.

"Don't—" I tried to warn them. *The wicked wicked man will drown the kids first, making you watch before he takes a blowtorch to the women's faces—I'm to pop his neck and kill him when he calls Pistol because he is bad.*

"Look," the woman said as she sat behind me, easing my head up gently to face forward, as if we were lovers, sitting in the park, watching our children play together. Heavy threw the cocaine that was in the bag up into the air, and it flew, catching itself, exploding into a spirit of white that held itself in the air. Each grain of white glistened like snow back home in a field of perfect light.

"We've been calling you home for years. We had to know it was you, but I knew. I knew it was you when I saw you." She kissed my forehead and her lips were burning with cold. "You've come home. Your family is waiting for you. Our children are waiting to be born with you."

Slim grabbed the second bag and walked to my right, doing the same. When he threw the cocaine into the air, it caught white fire and that's when I saw the wings blossom behind them.

"Angels," she whispered behind me.

The otters walked together to my left. They ripped open the third bag and they threw the cocaine up in the air, and before us three angels uncurled in the air. The mountain was east. The angels were around us in a circle of south, west and north.

I looked to the faces of the angels and they were looking at me with curiosity, waiting to see what I'd do. The wind gathered around me and I heard thunder again, this time closer.

"You are the way," the dragonfly lady whispered and knelt beside me, placing the drum she carried upon my chest.

I tilted my head and I felt something start to seep from beneath my fingernails. I coughed. "Cah...."

"You're going to come back as our leader. This woman is your wife. Your children are waiting for you. It is our time once more." She motioned to the woman behind me. I rolled my eyes up to look at her. My wife was now a red fox, crying. She brought something iron and sharp up, under my chin. The blade caught my stubble.

"Take our sickness with you," Dragonfly Woman said as she nodded to the fox.

"Wait—" I tried as she pulled. My skin split and blood sprayed out of me in a jet I heard slap my boots.

Dragonfly Woman took a long torch that had ignited from the fire and made her way past me. Hundreds of people with the faces of otters, goats, foxes, deer and bear now started to follow her. One by one they all took the reeds they were carrying and they dropped them onto the fire. Each reed went up, almost like a firework taking off. I heard Chumps start to whimper beside me. As the people walked away, they crouched and dropped to four legs, their skin becoming coats of fur, the firelight catching their silvery muzzles and throats.

"You're going to lead us all, husband," my future wife said as a red fox and kissed my forehead softly. "Do not fear this." My pant legs and shirt started to soak through with my own blood. I looked up and saw her sweet eyes looking down at me. Her breath was of sage, berries, smoke. Her muzzle twitched as a tear made its way down her snout. "You're going to take us home," she whispered and kissed me softly on the lips. Her cold nose brushed my face.

Heavy and Slim walked through the angel wings and stood on either side of me. Each pulled out a drum and started to play, singing the song they'd sung in the basement, "Ooooooo oo oh oooooo." And there was the design of the black wolf with light coming out of its mouth and eyes on both of them. I could see now that its body was being struck by lightning. This was the same design as the one on the drum that lay across my body.

A little otter wearing blue jeans came forward. He had an otter face but a human body. I saw his little brown tummy and nipples. He seemed afraid to speak to me but he held onto the large feather of a spotted eagle, which he touched to his forehead before kneeling. Our eyes met as he reached out and placed the feather in my hair. "I'm sorry I doubted you." He kissed me. "I'm sorry I didn't believe in you."

Son? *My son?* My wife as a red fox looked at me with tears in her animal eyes and nodded. She dipped her head and sent out a low call from her throat, a "whip whip" to our child. I looked and two small girls with the faces of foxes—the twin girls who'd been wearing dresses—stood behind their brother. They too held large, spotted feathers in front of their faces. They knelt by me, before taking my hands, their eyes catching the light.

"How?" I wanted to ask. "How can this be?"

"A deal was made for you," my wife said, touching my forehead with her wet nose. I felt her hot tears spread along my ears and neck. She began to wash my face with what smelled like tanned hide soaked in rain water.

"Come home, Papa," one of my girls said, brushing my arms with her feather, before she placed her hand over my heart. Thunder started to rumble above me.

"Take your skin off," the other said, brushing my chest with her feather. This was a washing ceremony. I knew this. It must have been to wash all my wickedness away. "I have missed you for so long."

"We're waiting for you," my boy whispered, sweeping his feather over my legs. He was strong. He placed my legs together like Jesus on the cross. They began to wash my throat and hands. With each sweep, the air felt cool upon me.

"The sky has to touch him first," my wife said, kissing my forehead so tenderly that tears filled my eyes. "All your life you've tracked us and now we're here." She looked up at the thundering sky and pulled the three hair ties off her wrist. "Come inside," she said to the children. "Sky fire is coming." She knelt, leaned close and tied all three feathers into my hair. "You are our resurrection." She kissed me softly on the lips. "You've been gone too long. Our children wait with me for your return. I love you. We love you. Our people wait."

My children started to wail. Long cries from the back of their throats and under their tongues. I heard them leave with their mother, taking their pitiful cries with them. Her cry was a low longing moan, deep from her chest, a trill of sorrow. How I wanted to comfort them all. But I was sinking inside.

I felt my hands rise from my sides as my vision started to fade. Sheet lightning arced over me as thunder tore the sky. The angel on the mountain turned to fire while the three angels watching me became a beautiful blue. The air sizzled and whipped around me. The people of the earth—earthworms— swam out of the ground and I could hear them whisper with their ancient tongues: *You are the way. You are the resurrection.* The grass charred and started to smoke around me as the electricity snapped and sizzled in the air above. The sky blackened. I could see stars.

The angel on the mountain exploded into fire. The three angels above me turned towards the city. I could feel their wings fanning me in hot drafts as they flew, and the earth trembled in their path. After them swarmed thousands more, and more, and with them their children. All of them held what looked like swords in each hand. Birds in the thousands swirled in clouds above me before bursting into horrific flame. And so did the mountain. All that beetle kill caught fire and began its way. I felt the earth rise up from under me to hold me, to cradle me, and I felt a heartbeat, the heartbeat of the earth, as I started to float. As my skin tightened, as my teeth fused, I finally—the sky had gathered for me. Flashes and flares started to pop and catch around me as my fingernails caught fire. I finally—a great rush blew through me. I closed my eyes and arched my back and the land became water. I finally—I started to sink and felt the hair on my body erupt with electricity, the feathers in my hair ignited to flames as a blue bolt from heaven tore through the sky towards me, blowing voltage through me, annihilating everything white. I was born a giant to become this—a child of something else—and, oh, my Maker, as I burst into flames I have finally found my way home....

Richard Van Camp

Don't Forget This

Long time ago, oh about ten years now I guess, there was this bush cook. You probably met her in your journeys. See if you can guess who she is, eh?

Well, all the time there were people at her house, eating, eating, eating. She cooked all day. And, well, if you brought her food she'd cook for you. She was on welfare so she was happy as long as her bills were paid and her daughter was fed and oh lots of stories, boy! Ever lots....

Well, she made this one friend, Shirley, we'll call her ('cause it's a secret). And Shirley, she bring Aunty lots of food: back strap, short ribs, kidneys—real traditional food as she has brothers who hunt. Aunty can tell Shirley is lost, like how insomniacs wander sometimes with their spirits walking three days behind them now....

So Aunty and Shirley they become close and Aunty can tell that Shirley is running from something—or maybe hiding. So! She goes out of her way to be good to Shirley 'cause Shirley loves Auntie's daughter, Mary. Mary loves Shirley and Shirley asks if she can baby-sit. For once now, Aunty has a babysitter she can trust and Shirley won't take her money 'cause she says being with Mary is enough. For the first time in so long, Aunty feels free. (Sssshhhh. She gonna look for a man!)

So she go out and have good time. (She found one on her first night now!) Oh she have a good time. That man sure know how to dance and use his hands and he smell so nice and sweet!

When she come home now, Shirley has the house cleaned and Mary is asleep in her bed. Shirley thanked Aunty for such a great night before Aunty can thank her and they become best friends.

So now every time after that, Shirley come over with a present for Mary. Sometimes toys, sometimes dolls, sometimes McDonald's. Aunty now, she don't have too much money to get stuff like that for Mary and she sees the way Mary's eyes light up when she gets toys like that, so what she do is she wait one night after Mary goes to sleep and she tell Shirley, "Shirley, you know you are my new best friend. I have to tell you. I'm so happy you look after my baby girl so good but it hurts me when you bring toys for her that I can't afford to get. I don't want my girl to think toys are love. I want her to know stories and family and friends and healthy food are love. We don't have lots of money, but we have a safe home and I'm proud of that."

"Oh, Aunty," Shirley said and covered her mouth, "I'm so sorry. Forgive me. I had a daughter once..." but she could not finish.

"I'm sorry," Aunty said. "I could tell you were hurting, but I didn't want to ask. What happened?"

"One time," Shirley said, "I had a good home: good man, good money, good town, and we had a daughter. Oh she loved to swim. So my Harold, he bring home a swimming pool one day and I didn't like it. Well, my girl loved it so what could I do? Well, she knows not to swim without me around. She knows that. One day, my show was on, and I was watching it. It was only a few minutes but that's all it took." She waved her hands in the air and the tears come now. "God took her." Oh those women they cry even harder.

"That's why when I see your Mary, I think of my girl. I never thought I would ever love again. Now I see her and I'm happy, me. I want to have another baby."

"Well, you need a man for that," Aunty said. And they burst out laughing.

"Well," Shirley said. "Maybe what we can do is help each other find hubbies. I'll baby-sit when you need help and you ask your boyfriend if he has any buddies."

"How did you know I had a man?" Aunty asked. Shirley pointed to her neck where she had a small hickey. And they laugh and hug and wipe each other's tears away and laugh again.

Well, everything went good for a month but the presents started appearing again and Aunty noticed that Mary was spending more and more time alone in her room. That's no good when there's company and everyone's telling good stories, so what she did was she got up and peaked into Mary's room and see that Mary has four new Barbie dolls that she'd never seen before. What made Aunty sad was she told Shirley she wanted to get the Olympic Barbie for Mary for her birthday but now she couldn't. Shirley beat her to it.

"Where did you get those dolls, my girl?" Aunty asked Mary.

Mary was scared and tried to tell her first lie: "I found them."

Aunty became so sad. Here was her girl trying to lie and she was only five. "Don't lie, my girl. Tell me."

"Well," Mary said. "Shirley gave them to me. She said I was her daughter now and that she was my real mom."

"What?" Aunty asked in shock. "What did you say?"

"Shirley is my real mommy," Mary said. "You are the lie."

Oh now Aunty got mad.

She took her girl by the hand.

"Let me go," her daughter said.

"Look," Aunty said as she pointed to the hallway of pictures she'd designed. "Look at all these pictures. This is you when you were a baby. You were one hour old here. Look, this is when you were baptized. Who's holding you? Me. There's your first day of school. There's when you lost your first tooth. Who held you? Who comforted you? Me."

Her girl shook her head. "No," she said. "My real mom said she was holding the camera and that she was only taking pictures of you because you're so lonely, you're so pitiful."

Richard Van Camp

Oh the breath left Aunty to hear this.

She put her girl to bed early and went into her bathroom and fell to her knees and she cried and prayed, cried and prayed. Shirley has been brainwashing her girl when she was babysitting her. This had all been an evil trick. She waited 'til Shirley come over that night to baby-sit and she gave her an earful. Aunty told Shirley to stay away from her daughter and that she didn't want her around the house anymore. Aunty was so hurt by what Mary told her that she could never forgive Shirley for lying to her girl like that.

"She's my girl!" Shirley yelled. "What kind of mother are you anyway? You don't have money. You never buy her what she wants. I can get her anything she wants. She doesn't even love you half as much as she loves me—"

Aunty slapped Shirley and yelled at her to get out of her house forever. Shirley did. She turned and she slammed the door but Mary went running after her. "Don't go, Mommy!" she yelled and Aunty could not believe her ears. Here, I guess, Shirley had told her that Aunty wasn't Mary's real mom and that Aunty was just babysitting Mary until Shirley could come and get her for real.

Oh, it was a sad time. Sad, sad time. Aunty told me she had to take Mary for help because her girl would not believe that she was her real mom and that Shirley was wrong for saying that.

Here now, Aunty goes to the police and gets a peace bond against Shirley. And now they are rebuilding their lives.

One night, a few weeks later, there was a knock at the door. It's the police. Aunty goes to the door and they say they need to talk to her. They say that Shirley's gone now. She's passed on so Aunty won't have to worry about her anymore. Aunty can't believe it! It turns out Shirley, she flip her car over the road and she was drinking. Sorry business... sorry, sorry, sorry business.

Oh, Aunty's sad. She can't believe it. How will she ever tell Mary? Well that night she have a dream. In this dream Shirley knocked on her door and asked to say goodbye.

"You passed on," Aunty said. "I heard you passed on."

"I have," Shirley said. "I came back to say I'm sorry. I'm at peace now and I asked to say sorry to you and Mary."

Aunty doesn't trust her and says, "Well, you go where you have to go now, but you leave us alone."

Shirley nodded and said, "I'll go, but can I give you a hug goodbye?"

And Aunty said okay.

So Shirley comes to Aunty and hugs her. "I'm so cold," she said. "Hold me."

Aunty holds Shirley and she's cold.

"I'm too cold to go," Shirley said and closed her eyes. "I just want to sleep."

"Shh," Aunty said. "You have to go now. Heaven's calling you."

"I know." Shirley lay on her side. "Come hug me one more time."

Aunty didn't like this and tried to stand but Shirley grabbed her. Boy, she was strong. She pulled Aunty down and held her so tight.

"What are you doing? Let go!"

"I'm so cold," Shirley said. "Just warm me and I'll let go. I promise. I'm too cold to leave."

Aunty tried to get away but realized that Shirley was too strong so she said, "Okay, okay. I will. I can't breathe. I'll hug you."

So Shirley let go and Aunty hugged her and they lay on their sides and Shirley was happy, "Oh I'm getting warm. I'm getting warm. Soon, I'll be strong to leave and go to heaven."

And Aunty didn't know what to do. She was hugging Shirley but she was so cold and, here now, she could feel struggling under her in the back of her mind. She didn't know what it was. Shirley felt it too and started to hug Aunty hard. "What is that?" Aunty asked.

"Nothing," Shirley said, "just hold me. I'm almost ready to leave."

But Aunty felt it again. Someone was under her and fighting to breathe. It was Mary!

Aunty used all of her strength and pushed Shirley off of her and opened her eyes. She was lying on top of her daughter who could not breathe! They had been smothering Mary!

Her daughter's lips were blue!

Luckily, Aunty knew CPR from all of her bush cook training and gave her daughter CPR and the whole time she was thinking, "Shirley came back for my girl!"

Thank God Mary lived but Aunty had to take her girl to the hospital.

"Why did you come to my bed, Mary?" Aunty asked her.

"Mom," Mary said. "I was so cold I couldn't get warm and someone told me to go lie beside you, so I did."

So that was a story she told me long time ago when I was eating at her house. Oh I got scared! That's why it's no good to bring kids around someone who just passed on or to bring kids around someone who's dying because, sometimes, even the dead get lonely.

Don't forget this.

The Power of Secrets

This one guy told me of a time in his life when he would go out with his flute to play in the forest, and a little porcupine shyly climbed out to the branch of a tree to watch him, one eye at a time, as the man played his heart out. I think this was in northern Ontario. This man told me he played for the little guy every day, and each day the porcupine came out on the same branch. It was a little game for them, hey. Well, one day this man was showing off and took a bunch of kids and the kids were loud and rowdy and so the porcupine came out but was very scared. He looked at the man only once with both eyes and what the man saw was so sad, as if the man broke something special.

The porcupine never came back.

The man felt such loss.

And that got me thinking, if you have something special that sometimes it's best to just keep it for yourself. Like if you fool around with someone, that's a good secret, hey? What you shared together was magic, special, fun. That's a good one. Your secret is held in two hearts. This will give you strength for the tough times ahead and when you see each other it's okay if you can't stop smiling. That's a good life, when you have a few of those. Not too many, though. I think if you fool around with too many honeys then you'll have weak kidneys. I think I heard that once. Weren't there some priests somewhere that thought if you don't ever fool around once that when they dig you up one hundred years from now that in between your rib bones there will be a pearl? It lets everyone know you were the patron saint of something. Well, I think that's a hard road, myself. Aren't we here to have a good time and help each other through the night? I think so.

Someone told me that Indians can only keep a secret for five years tops and then everyone spills the beans. Well, maybe that is true for all the races in our atmosphere: a five-year moratorium on the goods, hey.

● ○ ●

My friend, let's call him Freddy, told me one night that he was painting a drum and one of his co-workers called him.

"Hi, Freddy," Stella said.

It was late. He glanced at the clock. It was after eleven.

"Hi," he said. His son was asleep and it was a work day tomorrow. "Is everything okay?"

"Um, yeah," she said. "What are you doing?"

"Oh," he said. "Having tea, painting a new drum."

"Oh," she said. "I was wondering if you could come over and help me out."

"Help you out?" he said. "Everything okay?"

"Well…" she said.

"Is Sam giving you a hard time? Want me to come over there and tune him up?"

(Stella had been having problems with her ex, eh. The whole town knew about that.)

"Oh… no… no… Sam's outta town."

"What's wrong?" he asked. "Is your power out?"

"No… I was just wondering if you could come over and help me out?"

"Help you out," he repeated, putting his paintbrush down. "With?"

"Well," she said. "You know…."

And that's when it hit him: she was asking for help in the Love Me Tender Department.

"Oh!" he said. "Oh. Oh! Oh...."

"Well?" she asked with a smile that he could hear over the line.

"Oh, ah... whoah... Whew!"

"......"

"......!"

".....?"

".....!!"

"So?"

"So?" Freddy stood up. "So, ah, well, ah... my boy's asleep."

"So what? He can sleep on my couch."

"Oh well, ah, it's a school day tomorrow. I think they're taking pictures or something?"

"That's next month," she said flatly.

"Oh, well, ah... this is a bit sudden, isn't it?" Freddy asked. "I mean, well...."

"Sudden?" she asked. "For who?"

"Well, come on," Freddy said with his low secret voice. "We work together."

"So?" she said. "Just come over and help me out."

Freddy shook his head. He'd worked with Stella for over a year and, yes, they enjoyed each other's company. Yes, they shared a few good laughs, but he was so surprised.

"So?" she asked.

"I can't," he said. "Really...." He tried hard to think of what to say. "This is very flattering, but I don't think of you that way." This wasn't necessarily so. Stella had been hitting the gym pretty hard and was letting her hair grow out, so he'd had some Dirty Town thoughts these past few months.

"Oh come on," she said. "It'll be our secret. No one has to know."

"Ah," Freddy started pacing. "Ah. Ummm. Ah...."

"Please?"

"Oh that's so sweet," Freddy said. "But I have to say no. My son's sleeping."

"I could come over there," she said.

"*Ho-la,*" he said. "You're a brute, eh?"

"I can be," she giggled.

"No," he said with his whiny voice. "My son could wake up."

"I'll be quiet if you will," she said.

Freddy blushed. "Holy!"

"Come on," Stella said. "I could come over there and help you...."

At this, he started laughing and she started laughing, too. "Come on," she urged. "You've been on your own for how long now?"

"Oh," he thought about it. "Eight months now."

"And?"

"And what?"

"Don't you need a little help?"

Freddy's face flushed with embarrassment. He secretly called Stella The Hickey Monster as Sam's neck had always been covered in monkey bites or passion bruises when they were still married. And Freddy was no fashionista, but he knew that he was all out of turtlenecks. "Well, ah...." What could he say to that? "Well, I...." What could he say? "I, ah, am taking some time to take care of me...."

"And I could help," she said. "I could help you take care of you very nicely."

"I'm sure you could," he grinned.

It had been eight months all right. Eight months of learning to bake cookies for his son's fundraising events. Eight months of meetings with teachers and the optometrist to get glasses for his boy. Eight months of learning to cook supper and prepare sandwiches for his son's lunch every day. Eight months of waiting for his wife, to see if she'd ever return.

"Stella," he said. "I want to thank you for calling me. It's been a tough go."

"I can tell," she said.

"I'm really honoured that you called. Can I think about this?"

"You may," she said and she said it sweetly. Sometimes a woman can be tough on a man in a moment like this, but she could tell she'd disarmed him in a good way.

"I really need some time to think," he said. "I've been so focused on being a single dad and taking care of my boy that I've just gotten in touch with me."

"I'm really proud of you," she said. "You're a great dad."

"Thanks," he said. Because of his son's swimming lessons, Freddy had gotten over his own fear of the water. Because he was a single parent, he was now learning new recipes from his aunties. He could now cook a mean stir-fry and prepare salmon and halibut just the way his boy liked it.

"You're a real catch," she said. "I wanted to make my intentions clear."

"Well, they're greatly appreciated," he said. "Thank you."

"So?" she said. "Will you call me sometime when you know what you want?"

"I will," he smiled. "I will. I really want to thank you for the call."

"Okay, good night. It's nice to hear your voice."

"Yours, too," he said.

And she hung up softly.

And that was when Freddy decided that he wasn't waiting for his wife anymore. That was the night he decided that it was time to move on, that any woman who would leave her family behind without any explanation was a woman he could no longer trust for himself or for their boy, and that was the night Freddy went from being a passive good-hearted guy to an active participant in his life, a real mover and shaker.

So, did they ever get together? That's a secret. We just have to mind our own beeswax on that one. But let's get back to the spirit of this story: the medicine of secrets.

My buddy Trevor told me once that a long time ago the Crees used to go into the forest with a spear. And what they had to do was they'd sneak up on a bear and tap him on the bum with it—not the sharp side, but the flat side, I guess, and the bear would scoot away in fear. Then you would come out of the forest and never tell anyone about it. But that's what made you a man. If you could do that then you were a man. But the key was to never tell anyone, not even your wife. You keep it inside and you know it yourself, that you did that, hey.

So, my question to you all is do you have any secrets that you haven't ever told anyone? Good. Keep them inside you. If not, you better run out and start gathering some so they can keep you warm inside when you're in your golden years. The bad secrets should be talked about, I think, but the sacred ones, the special ones, the good time ones, I think you should keep them inside— not all, but some. Because they are medicine. They'll get you through the hard times. Plus, no one wants to fool around with you if they think you'll tell all your buddies and coworkers, hey! And whatever happened to kissing but not telling? Now that's a dying art (right up there with flirting, the four-hour makeout session and French kissing, in my opinion).

Me? I don't think I have too many secrets. Every five years I spill the beans to somebody about something, I'm sure, but I live a good life: I'm not out to hurt or take. The only secrets I have are my PIN numbers and the love songs that I sing into the wind for someone I haven't even met yet, but I know I will meet one day.

LOVE

Wolf Medicine: A Ceremony of You...

I have prayed you away for years but you've always come back stronger. It's in the way you laugh, the way you look at me, the way you suddenly become still when I tell stories, the way the world opens up for us when we're together. I should have listened to my own stories: sometimes when you pray for the Creator to keep someone away from you, He moves them into the middle of your heart. But this is what I want and it's time to tell you everything.

● ○ ●

I was surrounded by fire a long time ago. My grandfather spoke to me as he was dying. He said that his father told him a story. It went like this.

One winter afternoon my great-grandfather was out in the barrenlands hunting caribou. He was on his dog sleigh. As the dog team raced across the snow towards a bluff, they saw hundreds of caribou running towards them. To his surprise, his dogs raced away from the approaching herd. This was not their nature: the dogs were trained to run towards a herd so the musher could shoot as he rode.

But they turned away and were crying, screaming. He tried to whip the air around their ears to steer them towards the herd but they ran away as fast as they could. Oh the sounds they made were pitiful.

As my great-grandfather turned to watch the approaching caribou, he saw that they were not caribou: they were wolves, hundreds of wolves: tundra wolves, woodland wolves—wolves of silver, grey and black. Wolves of all shapes and sizes. They ran right past him and his team. They ran as if a fire chased them. His dogs all froze, crouching, bracing for attack, yet the wolves ran past them. My great-grandfather could only watch in awe.

As the last wolf passed them, he stopped. The wolf looked at my great-grandfather and told him two things.

The wolf told him of a ceremony that all the animals honoured for four days in the spring every year in the barrenlands. Each society met up there and spoke for four days: they spoke about what was coming in the wind, about their hardships, their joys, their families, their people. The others listened. And for four days there was no killing, only sharing. After that, the winged ones and the four-leggeds all raced back to their territories to resume the cycle of life for another year.

Then the wolf told my great-grandfather that he was watching the end of the four day ceremony for that year, and now that the wolf had locked eyes with a man to tell him this, the ceremony was broken: because a man knew what he was seeing now, the animals would not meet again this way, and this was a gift from the wolf people to our family, to make us stronger, to heal others, and that each time the animals give themselves to the people for medicine, all the animals suffer in sacrifice.

"You," my grandfather said to me, "have always been special. It was shown to me in a dream that when you choose your wife and have a child, the animals will meet again in the spring after your child is born. You will only have one. And your child will walk with the wolves. Your child will be a healer of healers and will not only work to unite the world but will also bring back the ceremony for the animals."

"Bring it back," Grandpa said. "The wolves in my dreams have asked you to find your mate, start your family, and call the world back into ceremony. We are in another world war. There's no caribou to be found. The oolichan have stopped running. It's time."

● ○ ●

I wanted to tell you all this, but that was the day you told me you were engaged. You looked so happy when you told me you could not imagine your life without him. I bit my tongue bloody when you told me about your wedding plans. I did not want to take away from your happiness, and the voices spoke: Let her go, the voices said. *Be stronger for her when she returns. You are needed elsewhere now....*

I think of those eyes of that last wolf and think of mine the night you got married as I put my fist through a window.

I told you something else about the scars on my fist but I was miserable for years after he took you away from me. I decided to be an ally for you and your husband rather than bring deception into your home. I did my best to meet your husband in a good way and become a friend, but I aged when I shook his hand, was weakened in the bones and lungs when I saw the way you looked at him in your home. I now understand how a cat can cripple someone who is working with bear medicine. I felt like a pipe carrier beginning a ceremony only to feel the crushing power of a woman on her moon—and it being too damn late to stop what had already begun.

I slept for a year after you married him, confused. How could this be? In my dreams it was always you. Maybe I was wrong. Maybe the wolves were wrong. This was the power I wanted to share with you.

Let her go, they said. *Be stronger for her when she returns. You are needed elsewhere now....*

That's all I had to go on, so I vanished into the world as a helper.

Richard Van Camp

● ○ ●

I knew what my grandfather meant when he said I was special. When I was a child we were caught in a blizzard out on the land and made our way to see an old trapper and his wife holed up in their log house. I was about four. We barely made it before the wind and the snow struck the land hard. It had been so cold for so long that many of the trapper's huskies had died, and he let the others stay in the back porch where it was heated.

"No matter what," the old timer said, "don't let your son go in that back room. Those dogs are mean."

The wind howled outside around us as we sipped tea and ate dry caribou meat. I was four and curious. This was the first time I heard the voices: *Go to them*, they said. *Go see the dogs.* I looked around, thinking the adults could hear this. But they were laughing away, telling stories, sipping their tea. *Go to them*, the voices said. *Trust us.*

As my parents got into their visiting, I asked to go to the bathroom. I was shown where to go and made my way, past the bathroom, down the hall. As I made my way towards them, I wanted to see the dogs. *Behind the door*, the voices said. *They're waiting for you.*

It was like being guided by many hands. I walked into the porch and they were sleeping. Oh I could smell them: earthy and luxuriant. *Go to the leader*, the voices said. *Show him who you are.* My heart was pounding as I shut the door behind me and walked through them towards the leader. He was different. I could tell he was mostly wolf. *This one has spirit eyes*, the voices said. *He can see what the others can't.*

I walked though the sleeping huskies, made my way quietly past them and held my hand out until I touched the leader's nose. At that, he jumped up with a start—terrified by the insult. The other huskies surrounded me, giving low throaty growls to each other to kill, but I wasn't scared. I peeled my lips back to reveal my own teeth and flicked my tongue along them, radiating with power, and I let out a growl from under my tongue that made them back away, tails between their legs, ears back, crouched. When the adults found me, the huskies and the wolf leader were bowing to me, and I was smiling....

That was the day seven wolves surrounded me and began to guide my life.

● ○ ●

I danced for joy when I heard your husband cheated on you. I danced. I prayed. I sang. I jigged in the rain. I jigged in the snow. I jigged in the middle of my street at four in the morning because I knew you were free.

And now here we are: in Vancouver and free....

But I don't want to be just friends any more. I want to be lovers. I want us to claim Vancouver and all of her territory as our own. I want our son to know this place, these great people, the mountains, the ocean, the land.

I have prayed about this, and this ceremony of you came to me in a dream. Years of training on the hill, seeing my sisters through cancer, gaining strength to face the circle of Tlicho elders, helping the people, living for others, becoming a road man—all of this was done to put you out of my mind, but you're free now and we can be together. This is our time and I'm strong enough to hold you in a good way. This is our time now, but we have to be careful because I don't want to lose what we have. It's time to welcome you to your home in me.

This is what our wolves showed me:

Let's meet at JJ Beans on Main and 14th. We can have coffee. You need to look into my eyes so you see that I can be trusted with your life. Wolf medicine is the only way to build on what we have and for me to welcome you into my heart as my mate.

Richard Van Camp

Let us meet in a new way. Please bring me a pouch of tobacco; Red Man is best as it was my grandfather's favourite. Please bring me a piece of your favourite clothing, as well, unwashed. It has to hold your scent, your memory....

After, when it's dark, we will go back to my place. I will shower first. You are welcome to look around. I'm sure you will see the picture of my grandparents sitting together. Look into their eyes: see the majesty. Do your very best to open yourself into the wisdom they see, even from the other side. They asked about you before they passed. They looked away when I told them you were married because they could see the tears in my eyes. They said they would pray for you and maybe they did. Maybe they prayed you back to me.

On this first night, you can put on any music you like. You are welcome to bring your own. Then you will shower. You must be careful not to wash your hair. We can't lose your scent. Please don't wear any perfume. I don't want you to wash your hair the morning or day you see me.

I will lie down in my bed first, under the blankets. Don't worry: I'll have a T-shirt and underwear on. After you shower, you will come into my room and you should wear a T-shirt.

You will lie on the right side of the bed. I will lie on the left. Come into my arms. The way I will hold you is I will lie on my left facing you. You will lie on your right facing me. Come into me and let me work wolf medicine on you.

I'm going to start by kissing your forehead and your temples. I'm going to then smell the very top of your head and your temples, for this is where your scent is. I'm going to inhale you deep so I can see your secrets. This is how I'll see you as a little girl. I'm going to drink in the images that I see. I'm going to see you with hope in your eyes, waiting, waiting for me to come pick you up, getting ready for a dance, eating with your family. You won't be able to hide much from me so don't even try. Words won't matter anymore when I have you like this and, soon, I'll see everything. I'll watch how you've seen me grow as a man, and I will see what I have to change in myself to become more than I've ever been to you before.

This is how wolves dream when they choose their mates and I want to do this with and for you. It's important that your hands don't wander because if they do, the ceremony will be broken. Let's get over the temptation to make love just yet. Please respect me about this.

I'm allowed to kiss you, but you cannot kiss me. Your job is to be honoured, nuzzled and kissed. If you kiss back or caress, you'll fall into the role you've been playing and I'll be like every other lover who's been there before me. Let's not do that.

I want to inhale you.

I'm going to caress you and I'll keep my hands in the PG zones: small of your back, your shoulders, your neck. Again, I'm allowed to kiss you but you can't kiss back. If you kiss back, the circle will break.

We are going to do this for four nights. Each morning we will watch the sunrise and you will tell me everything you remember about your dreams. Don't leave anything out. The wolves who guide me will have listened and whispered to us during our sleep.

I'll need each of these four days for myself. I'm going to drop tobacco in the places throughout the city that hold *neezee inkwo*—good medicine—for us. The wolves will have shown me all of these places in my dreams. I'm going to spend my days praying and sensing what to do next, rolling your dreams and answers through my mind, thinking, seeing. I'm going to be praying about you and your life and I'm going to sleep and dream like my grandfather and great-grandfather. Your favourite piece of clothing will be under my pillow, tucked into my pillowcase, and your world will be revealed to me through the spirit of it when I dream.

If you hear drums while you are at work or smell the earth, wood smoke or mint around you, don't worry: that's me praying for you. Welcome it. Welcome everything that comes your way.

Richard Van Camp

All I ask is you go to the ocean for at least an hour every day and listen to what your blood tells you. Then, I want you to make a fire. I want you to cook a feast for seven wolves and my family. I want you to burn it all. This is what we call feeding the fire. I also want you to burn two plugs of Old Man chewing tobacco for my grandparents. As you do this, your ancestors will meet mine. I ask that you do this on the first day.

There is a yellow dog with red eyes waiting for you on the corner of Gore and East Cordova. On the second day I want you to go to him and look into those red eyes. Bring him tobacco. Lay it before him and pray. Pray for our future. Pray for our son. Speak all you are asking for out loud in me so the spirits can help you. You can share with me what you wish when you come back later that evening.

On the third day, feed the fire for your family. You will have a fever. This is because you are now becoming more spirit than human.

On the fourth day, feed the fire for us. By now, you should hear whispers around you faintly. Your sense of smell will be heightened and you're going to sense things far more easily. Trust everything that you feel. If the earth wants to, let her take you alive. I can wait until you return.

It's your job to fall asleep in my arms. If I wake you up in the middle of the night, you're to let me kiss the back of your neck and place my leg between yours as we spoon. No matter what happens, we are not to make love. If I wish to kiss or breathe against your neck, you are not to give in. It's when you feel the feathers or the soft fur move against you that you can't open your eyes. This is when I need you to trust me the most because that's when I'll pass on your wolf medicine. Three of the wolves who guide me have called your name. They've asked me to come to you as a gift.

● ○ ●

There was a hunter who once saw my grandparents walking together, though my grandmother was walking with a tundra wolf, caressing the fur on his back as they walked. I want you to know this kind of magic again… the way you used to… when we were kids and still believed in the possibilities of the world.

● ○ ●

For four nights we are going to honour you and all you've been through. Let your scent and the memory in your blood show me what happened along your trail of light. I'm going to travel through your life and braid your scars with ribbons of light. Every place you've left your spirit, I'm going to gather it for you. Every person who ever harmed you will be dealt with, and any approaching sickness will be burned away….

For four nights we will do this. If I have questions, I want you to think very carefully about the answers. Your instinct will be to answer quickly, but I want you to give yourself permission to take as long as you need to. If you need a day or two to think about your response, that's fine. Your job is to answer honestly—maybe honestly for the first time to anyone.

You are welcome to ask me questions on the sunrise of our new life together. I am willing to take the chance of losing you as a friend and welcoming you back as a mate for life, and this is the way I was shown to do it. All this for the girl who told me she invented horses before she kissed me for the very first time. All this for the girl who skated into my heart at fourteen. All this for the only woman I was ever born for.

Let's make medicine for the world through our love.

It's time to raise a healer of healers and put the world back into ceremony.

Come into the heart of me

Richard Van Camp

and let's make this city ours to roam,
for each other
for our family
for the world....

Idioglossia

U,

Currently reading: *Forbes 400 Richest* (for our burial suits), *Spin* (though thoroughly disappointed with their articles on Radiohead and PJ Harvey as they were way too short and lacking anything important) and stories of non-consent.

Last poem written:
Watching you with the bloody eyes of a dog. Pornography is about force and I need all the force I can get. The intimacy of shame... God I love it.... Let your cum motor roar, baby, and come screaming clear....

Saddest realization: I know that the antibiotics stain my teeth yellow and stain yours white while antidepressants make me gain while you lose weight. The Interferon helped you quit smoking and took the hair off your ass, while it left me tired all the time and full of regret (so unfair).

Latest regret: Should not have turned on the light to find the Thai beads as it scared Tina and Rena into leaving. They had no idea our bodies were so wasted and starving (mostly mine). Plus, when we were in London, we should have ordered our driver to pull over and take us to the Touch Museum (Museum for the Blind, remember?).

In this spoken moment: I speak but am unspoken to, have the wrong sometimes chemicals inside me (between 3 pm and 4 am), still have painful bouts thinking about the pinkest and softest in duplicities.

What I remember most about Ocho Rios: Our Jamaican bodyguard's back. It looked like the face of a vampire bat, so heavily muscled and cut. I was so proud of him and thought that I, at the time, was pleased with his work.

Top or Bottom? Behind.

Fashion sense? Leather's out. Love's in. A man is not complete without a belt. Dreadlocks look like dog hair, and we detest hemp.

White dogs = Death comforters. They're in my dreams everywhere, and that's why you wake up crying.

Most wonderful friend? Isn't it obvious?

Most inspiring movie? *Chinese Ghost Story 1*. It's the perfect love story. Really.

Most chilling Christmas carol that scared us (me more than you): "You better not shout/ you better not cry/ you better not pout/ I'm tellin' you why…."

Last kiss with mild tongue: At the airport, yesterday. You'll never guess who. (Okay, it was Rhonda. Are you mad?)

Most inspiring book intro: *The Lover*. Read it to me over and over and over.

Best alternative to coffee: cappuccino.

Worst pick up line: "We were wondering what the view from your bedroom window's like" (Can you believe *that* worked?).

Strangest neighbours growing up: Patrick and Huey. No last names as we recall. Always lighting things on fire and jacking each other off. Both were uncircumcised so their peenees looked like nightmare creatures that were somehow captured but always shy. The brothers kissed. With tongue. They had pink eyelids and hair so white it glowed in the dark. One had asthma; both were bad seeds. They fucked us up!

Best secret joy: My collection of throwing knives. Plus, the feeling when we are sharks on Zadaxin weaving our way through three-lane traffic: me in my Jag, you in yours.

Biggest toy question: Where do all the old toys go? Back to Taiwan, or what?

Fave drink: Old Tyme Jamaican Ginger Beer though the Australian Ginger Beer is better. (Note to ourselves: Must find out brand name in Sydney, Oz, and see if they import to Canada using kegs. Further, call Jamaican bodyguard and get him to fuck you-know-who up some more. Get him to use the bathtub this time and let them scream underwater.)

Chronic all time fear: Being vomited on in public and it's hot and I have to walk all the way home without you.

Funnest time in hospital (so far): When my appendix blew a week to the day yours did and we had to share Room 4. (I still don't believe the night nurse went down on you, silly boy.)

What keeps me awake lately: Ever since you told me there are blood stains in every ballerina's right shoe. (As always, I just have to see it for myself). I imagine the purple stain inside the first shoe I inspect is the purple our palms have become, is the darkening black of our livers.

Favourite picture: You and me in the parkas Mum made us. Snow falling. We can hear each other grow at night.

Best idea for a web site that will make us our second million: www.o-faces.com. People will send in their orgasm faces to us, hopefully more women than men as men look like they are doing something violent and wrong or as if they have just been murdered by their best friend and are thinking, "Of all people—you?" There will be no consoles, no blink links, no bullshit. We'll show the ecstasy, show the open mouth closed eyes "bring me thunder so hard I see lightning" look, show the "Oh my God you're inside me and you're magnificent and stronger and fucking me harder than my mother has ever been fucked and I love it and it's like I'm riding a horse upside-down and I'm shaking I'm shivering I'm bucking and my legs are over your shoulders and I can feel your bad boys smack against me!" look.

Fourth saddest affliction: I'm getting those tiny polyps or cell formation or whatever they call them on my neck and I strongly feel that it is our laundry soap transferring contamination through my collar. I see this affliction on other men everywhere and feel like we are a growing tribe. You, of course, are beautiful and immune.

Strange urge: To get you stoned thru hash cookies which other bi-curious twins have baked together.

Best feeling: My Levi's 100% cotton V neck T-shirt and my boxers you bought me for Mother's Day, coffee (three creams, brown sugar) in the moon and stars mug you got me for Christmas, Saturday (any season), fresh haircut, (I can feel the breeze against the back of my neck and I feel like Velcro). You walk in, your enchanting smile, the Jag's gas tank's full, vacuumed interior, my clear skin, great tunes that make me remember I'm not second best, filed nails, nasal passages clear (no blow or cheese the day before), new knife, no pills needed, it's our birthday, the laundry's done, you've ironed my shirts, my warm 501's in the dryer, and you hug me before we even say hello and when we do it's in Dypthia, our secret language, our secret way, our language of forever, the language only twins know.

Honest truth: I tried touching you-know-whose hand when you were fucking her on the top bunk and I was on the bottom. Couldn't you remember I had written my first ever love letter that said: "I have only one thing to say: (turn the page) I love you I love you I love you I love you I love you I love you I love you I love you." I mean it's okay—I just wish you had waited....

Most fascinating thing about our hepatitis is it fascinates me about as much as people who have never had nosebleeds, dentists who've never had fillings, or people who have only seen televised snow.

Final wish: If you die without me, can you just please think about me when you leave and remember us as children? You know I won't be far behind.

Breath of fresh air: If you add up both our years, we've now retired and we're old and feeble and we can get bunk beds again when we start to get really sick. Who knew all our suck-and-fuck tours would come to an end in the feast of our hunger in Ocho Rios? Let Jamaica eat itself. Yeah, those twins knew they had something. They must have.

I get top bunk this time (or you can, if you're going to pout). We'll just pretend it's our appendicitis again but that it's spreading and we'll beat this thing with our Autoimmune Twin Power of Wound Healing.

Richard Van Camp

Last Rites: Bury us in Fort Smith. I want Amazing Grace by Daniel Lanois on repeat. I want to be buried with you. I can't believe we turned 30 a week ago. I want for us peace and quiet forever together alone and to whisper in Dypthia, *We were gorgeous. Everyone said so. We were never ashamed of our beauty. I love you I love you I love you I love you I love you I love you I love you I love you.*

Love always,

U2

A Darling Story

Our love has made us old, Lance thought as he sank back into the couch and adjusted the bag of frozen peas in his track pants. Oh he was swollen and tender. It felt like the surgeon had stomped on both of his testicles before stuffing them back inside his scrotum six months and a week earlier. And every day they swelled until the pain was beyond agony.

"You good?" Duane asked.

Lance winced and nodded as he shifted in his seat and waited for the hash brownies to cradle him, to sink him into the couch and vanish him for the night. "Where did we get this?"

Duane lit another candle. "Compassion Club."

Lance let out a long breath and watched the candlelight flicker on the walls. "I thought you needed a doctor's note or something."

"That's Compassion on Wheels. Compassion Club doesn't care."

"They come all the way out to White Rock?"

Duane ran his hands over Juanita's hips and kissed her gently. "They do."

Supper had been magnificent but quiet. Duane and Juanita had prepared a salmon feast that could have fed three more couples: there was also baked halibut, fresh potatoes, corn and a salad that Shari had put together in the way only she could. Juanita kept glancing at Shari, and Duane, the peacekeeper, had done his best to raise everyone's spirits by talking about what they had learned at the couples retreat. Lance had tried to keep up but the gnawing agony between his legs and the wall of resentment between him and Shari had been too much. He had faded in and out of the conversation, stirring his food rather than eating it.

Duane was Gitxsan. He was an architect and slowly making a name for himself in the industry. Juanita was Haida and was in line to take over as vice-principal at a local elementary school. Both Duane and Juanita volunteered with various Downtown Eastside causes. This, somehow, was their ticket into the hash brownies situation, Lance thought. They had a gorgeous townhouse. Their home was filled with the artwork of Roy Henry Vickers, Chris Paul, Susan Point, and George Littlechild. There were plants everywhere and Lance inhaled deeply, picturing himself breathing pure vitamins. Lance watched Duane and Juanita lean into each other as they hugged. *They're going to have beautiful children,* Lance thought before glancing at Shari, but Shari looked away, tucking her feet under herself.

"So how are you two doing?" Duane asked.

"We're sorry about the news," Juanita said and looked directly at Lance.

Lance felt the heat of the buzz start in his fingers. Over the four years that he and Shari had known Duane and Juanita, they had become closer. They were allowed to ask. Lance and Duane were sweat brothers. The Dogrib did not sweat, but Lance was one of the helpers. He and Duane had shared many conversations about their partners as they helped prepare the feast and sweat at UBC. He let Shari field this one.

"We're coasting, hey, Lance?" Shari said. It wasn't a question. Her cut hair only accentuated her sharp Dene features and Lance closed his eyes because it was too painful to look at her and not be able to touch her or comfort her. The distance between them was too thick, too fiercely protected, and they had run out of words for each other. She had not spoken to him on the hour-long ride out here. Lance had watched Vancouver sweep into Richmond and Richmond grow into fields. He'd seen horses, and felt a quiet peace knowing the ocean was to his right.

Lance thought of Duane and Juanita. They'd just returned from a rediscovery camp for couples and couldn't stop kissing each other. *They have found their way*, he thought. *And we have lost ours.* Lance wanted to reach for his coffee but couldn't. Ever since he learned that the six-month reversal test was a bust, he was now back on the coffee in a big way. He had been sipping tea from his acupuncturist that tasted like bog water that was supposed to promote fertility, but that was all gone now that his infertility was confirmed. Each sip of coffee now seemed to lighten the sorrow he felt in his bones for a little while.

Since the reversal, his orgasms had grown stronger, but he hadn't told anyone—not even Shari. There was a team of people who'd been cheerleading them on: his doctor, his surgeon (who was the best in the province), his acupuncturist, his homeopath, their couples counsellor, his counsellor, her counsellor, his friends (Duane being the head cheerleader), his brother, her friends (he assumed mostly Juanita), her sister, their friends—and the team all agreed on two things: 1) he had to start talking to Shari about this; if he didn't, he'd lose Shari; 2) Shari had to forgive him for something he did long before he met her. She had to or she'd lose him.

"The road to pregnancy can either make or break a couple," his acupuncturist said. "Sometimes the wish is not the reality. The key is you have to talk through it. You have to do the good hard work, and you have to do it together."

The good hard work, Lance thought. All talk of buying a home together was frozen; all talk of a traditional marriage was off; what used to be a full fridge of groceries was now littered with a few basics. Lance often ate alone.

"I'm scared," he whispered and closed his eyes.

"What?" Shari asked.

"He's stoned," Duane said.

"I feel like a broken horse," he said.

"Cheap date, Lance," Shari said. "This party's for you." And there was that edge, that how-could-you tone, as he called it.

Lance sank into the couch and started to drift. He'd scoffed when he caught Shari sneaking a puff every once in a while at parties or outside a pub, and he'd refused to join her at Duane and Juanita's when they hosted hash brownie parties, but, after the urologist suggested adoption or sperm donation, Lance pretty much surrendered to depression. They'd learned together that the scar tissue from his vasectomy was too thick and that nothing life-creating could get through. Lance had this vision of squeezing semen through a scissored fortress of bone spurs every time he ejaculated. And, worse, he now had an infection of some kind. Something was trying to squeeze through the scar tissue and it was agony.

"Bring on the hash cookies," he'd said to Duane when he called to see how things were. And he and Juanita gladly obliged.

Lance had gotten a vasectomy during his first marriage when he told himself that any children would be an absolute burden, a never-ending series of chores and doom, a life of thankless duty, a kiss goodbye to anything luxurious. Truth be told, his ex-wife, Larissa, did not want children. Her upbringing had been terrifying. After four years of watching her try every form of birth control, it was apparent that her system was too fragile to handle anything more. She had a latex allergy; foam was like paint remover to her; she tried five different kinds of the pill, and Depo made her "bipolar" for the six months she felt it leaching through her blood stream. And her terror became his. He sank within himself and let himself remember for a second the dread around "period time." If Larissa was a day or two late, there would be no sleep, tears, terror. It was during the horrible afternoon when her IUD had implanted itself into her uterine wall and became infected that Lance made up his mind. Sitting in his car on a rainy afternoon outside St. Paul's Hospital as Larissa underwent day surgery, Lance decided that he would get a vasectomy. He did not want to bring a child into the world with the woman he loved if she did not want a baby. What he did not know was that Larissa was having an affair with a colleague. What was worse was she let him go through the operation while cheating on him. Crueler still was that Larissa and her colleague were now parents: they'd had twins.

His divorce had ruined him. He spent the first eight months on his couch watching movies, crying into a towel he kept close by. No words from family or friends helped. He felt alone. Worse, he could not imagine anyone wanting to be with him ever again now that he was sterile.

A year after his divorce was finalized, he'd met Shari and that all changed. Shari was what he'd always wanted but thought he'd never find: Chipewyan, a northerner who knew who she was and where she came from, ultra-feminine from a family of matriarchs, a woman who was born to create a home for a family. Growing up in Lutsel'ke, she was learning her language and culture and was a master weaver of both cedar and birch bark. Her grandparents were medicine people, "the last of the chanters" as she'd once told him. She had been married before to a Gitxsan and had lived in Hazelton for some time. She was working on her PhD and they'd met on campus.

Lance taught storytelling and was working on his PhD as well. They'd met and moved in together within a year and a half and, after two years of living together and discussing a traditional marriage and having a family, Lance had gone for the reversal. At first, Shari was a saint. She'd been a great nurse after the operation and had gone beyond the call of duty, but, after his first test, six weeks after his reversal, when the urologist said the results showed no movement and that the tubes were still swollen, something changed in her. Immediately. They'd gone home together in the car and she was quiet, so deeply quiet. Lance pleaded with her to say something, putting his own terror on hold. "Please baby. Say something."

She stared straight ahead as she drove, her cheeks flushed into fierce blades of red. "What do we do now?" was all she asked. And that was when the silence in Lance crept inside of him, and the fear. Fear that he was powerless, powerless in that what he'd decided for Larissa was now final for him and Shari. The next morning, Shari had called in sick and left for the day, leaving Lance filled with dread. When she returned that night, she had cut off her long hair and moved like an old woman. Every trace of anything to do with a baby was put into the nursery room they had prepared together and the room was locked. All the picture frames celebrating babies, the little moccasins she had made—everything was gone. She stared through things and retreated into a world of deep misery.

"She is grieving her dream," Greg, his counsellor, told him. "Are you?"

Lance could only stare at his hands. He had retreated so far inside himself that he had no words for anyone when they questioned him directly about how he felt. He'd freeze. He'd freeze when he was talking about it with Shari; he'd freeze when he was talking about it with his acupuncturist; he'd freeze when he tried answering anyone. He would have no problem when he started the conversation, but direct questions locked him up.

Lance began to float a whisper above his body and the buzz bloomed behind his cheeks. He could feel a luxurious heat lift off his ears and he didn't care if the sun rose tomorrow or not. No. He was sterile and had an infection of some kind. He was sitting on a bag of frozen peas and it felt like he had three swollen balls. Shari resented him for his past life. The cold fear of his future had gripped him completely on the way home in the car after his three-month test result when the urologist had sat them down and said, "The tubes are still not clear."

"How do I build a home without children?" Shari had thrown her hands up and started crying in the car. "How do I live without children? Why was I born if I can't be a mother? Why? You tell me, Lance. I'm piggybacking my future on your past with that white bitch, and she has twins with the man she cheated with. Where's the justice in that?"

Lance froze once again and looked down. "I'm sorry," was all he could say.

"What are you apologizing for?" she'd asked. "I don't need an apology."

"Well, what do you need?" he had asked, confused.

"I need you to make it right!"

"Shari, I'm doing the best I can."

"Well, it's not working, Lance. It isn't. Fix this for us. You need to fix this and you need to fix this right now. And I need you to bloody well talk to me."

"I don't know how to fix this, okay? I do not know."

"Well, can I just be a bitch and ask why the fuck you didn't bank some sperm?" She started crying into her hands.

Lance held her and rocked her gently. "Because I didn't know I'd meet you, okay? I didn't know. How could I know?"

"Why do they get to have a family and we don't?" she'd asked and started crying again. "It's not fair, Lance. I want a family for us. It's all I want now."

"Me too, baby," he said and cried with her. "Me too."

And that was when Shari had started wearing pyjamas to bed. They'd stopped making love. That was when she stayed out later with Juanita. They had found a women's circle that involved sweats and spiritual retreats. Juanita and Shari had gone together. Often, she would come home smelling of cedar and sweet grass, but she would not talk about where she had been for the weekend or what they were doing. Shari would return strong for a few days but then she would get this look, this sadness, and move slowly again. She had also started sleepwalking. Lance found her a few mornings sleeping in the nursery room that they had prepared together. She'd be on the floor, wrapped in a blanket she had made for the baby. That was by far the worst for Lance: to see the pain he had brought to someone who had earned the right to a beautiful life. He hated himself for what he had done to Shari. And that was when he'd stopped trying to feel. He'd lose himself in movies, video games, online porn. Anything to feel like a man.

He held onto something he'd read at the urologist's clinic: that a man needed to ejaculate every three days to create and maintain healthy sperm. The word *virility* had never mattered to him before, but it was his mantra all the time now. *Virility, virility, virility.* He hated himself and his decision to burn the bridge, to cauterize the tubes that could give them what they both wanted now: a family.

She's biding her time to leave, he thought. *I have failed her. And she's rejected me. And there's nothing more I can do.* He remembered words that their couples counsellor, Wanda, had said: "The number one reason marriages and partnerships fail is failed expectations. When a life-changing event like infertility comes up like this, you can either fall apart or you can fall together. It will always come down to communication." Lance bristled at how hard the past six months had been. "I'm a eunuch," he said.

Juanita burst out laughing. "What?"

"I'm a eunuch," he repeated and the room fell quiet. He never wanted to open his eyes again.

"Easy," Duane said.

"And now my orgasms are strongest in doorways," he confessed.

"What?" Shari asked, alarmed.

It was true. Whenever he had to ejaculate for a sperm count or to maintain virility or just to feel magnificent for as long as he could, he got down on all fours and discovered that any time he came halfway through a door that his orgasms were beyond physical. They were metaphysical, loud in the soul.

"And I'm not a chronic masturbator. A man should ejaculate every two to three days to maintain a healthy sperm count."

The group laughed. Even Shari.

This felt good. He could feel waves of weight leave his body. He wanted to reach for more hash brownies and chase it down with his beloved coffee. He knew there were two brownies and half a cooling cup of coffee left, but he could not move. He started to drift around the room, as if he were having an out of body experience. The throbbing pain between his legs now hummed to a dull buzz.

"Did I tell you," Shari said, "that my old soccer ball contacted me today on Facebook?"

"What?" Duane and Juanita asked.

"What?" Lance echoed, delayed in his response time.

Shari sat up. "When we were kids, my mom brought us home a soccer ball she'd found one day. On it in huge letters was the name Nelson Crummy. We fell in love with this soccer ball. We took it everywhere—to the lake, out to restaurants. And we'd all say, 'Hey, where's Nelson Crummy? Has anyone seen Nelson Crummy?' Even my parents got into it. 'Well, Nelson Crummy,' my father would say, 'what do you feel like for supper tonight?' 'I think Nelson Crummy wants barbeque chicken with corn on the cob and baked potatoes,' Mom would say."

She stopped to take a sip of water. Lance felt something lift inside of him. As Shari had started this story, he got a glimpse of her family when they were younger, running in black and white, laughing together, not kicking the ball but running and passing it to each other in a field of tall grass. Her muddy hands, her marvelous feet in little shoes.

"Holy shit!" Duane yelled. "That's like that Tom Hanks movie—what was it called...."

"*Castaway!*" Juanita said. And they started laughing.

"What?" Shari asked.

"The ball that Tom Hanks has as a best friend. Wasn't his name—Wilson?"

"Yeah," Juanita said. "Holy cow, this is just like that."

"Did we see that movie?" she asked Lance.

Lance frowned. He had watched it with Larissa. "I don't think so. Go on, sweetie."

She looked at him with surprise. He hadn't called her that in months. She continued. "And it went on and on. We couldn't leave the house without Nelson Crummy. We played with Nelson Crummy and the thing is he kept leaking, so we had to keep pulling over to every gas station we came across and my dad didn't mind. My mom didn't mind. Nobody minded. And we loved it. We loved it all. Then one day my mom came home and Nelson Crummy was gone. She'd met Nelson Crummy—the boy. The one whose ball it was. He was in her class. She'd noticed his name on her class list and confessed to him that his ball, his name, his very spirit had traveled with us across Canada all summer. He seemed unimpressed. All he cared about was getting his soccer ball back, so she gave it back—though we were all pretty sad about it. Even my dad."

"Cheap," Duane said. "So what happened?"

"Well, it was right after that that we had the fire and lost everything."

"Oh, sweetie," Juanita said. "Did you add him as a friend?"

"I did," she said and Lance tried to frown about this. He tried to frown but wasn't sure he could move his face anymore. He was really stoned. But he had seen her. He'd seen Shari's life.

"Well, that's a sad story," Juanita piped. "Who needs water?"

"All of us, sweetie, please," Duane said.

Lance listened with everything inside of him and he opened his eyes. His eyelids felt thick and sticky. There was Shari curled on the couch. She'd taken her socks off and he could see her feet. Her beautiful Dene feet. It was her feet that had closed the deal for him when they started dating but he'd never told her. Her toes were delicately shaped, each one a jewel to massage. Like amber beads. Her ankles, her feet, her toes, the muscles and perfection of her feet revealed themselves to him every time they used to go out because the night would truly begin with Shari asking for a foot massage. He'd gladly oblige and he remarked once that she used a certain red polish that drove him crazy. She'd apply it for him every Friday and they'd never make it out the door for supper or a night on the town. He hadn't massaged her feet or toes in weeks now.

She hadn't painted them either. She'd also taken off the silver toe ring Lance had given her after their six-month anniversary.

She'd taken off her ankle bracelet that she used to wear. Lance came home to find them gone and, just like the haircut and the locked nursery, he knew not to ask about it. He and Shari were becoming strangers, but in this story about the soccer ball, there she was—that girl he adored. She'd lost her family photo albums in a house fire and he'd spent hours—days really—trying to imagine her as a girl, as a young lady, as a teenager. There were no pictures of her that he'd ever seen and this was magic because when she'd told this story, he could see flashes of her life: her brother, her sister, her parents. For some reason, they were all wearing suits in this story. For some reason, this story was in black and white. For some reason, their hair was matted down with something. And he saw Shari with bad perms, awkward dresses, friends who'd moved on, sleepovers. He'd seen the memory of birthday cakes and pizza parties. He'd glimpsed a movie reel of Shari growing up.

"I love that story," Lance said, fascinated. "What was his name?"

"What?" Shari asked.

He sat up slowly. "What was the soccer ball's name?"

"Nelson Crummy."

He felt a heat spread between his legs as he imagined her tanning, learning how to dance, laughing, kissing for the first time.

"What?" Lance asked again.

Shari looked at him with suspicion. "Nelson. Crummy."

Lance felt something more: he felt the heat spread within his thighs through his balls.

"One more time," he said.

"Why?" She asked.

"Please," he said and motioned with his eyes towards his lap. "Baby. Please. Say it one more time."

"No!" Shari said, but she said it playfully.

"What's going on over there?" Juanita asked.

"You okay, buddy?" Duane asked.

"Yeah," Lance said and looked at the group. He was looking at Shari and Shari was looking at him.

Richard Van Camp

"Do you need more peas?" Duane asked. "We have more."

"No," Lance said. "I just want to hear his name again."

"Nelson Crummy!" the group bellowed and everyone burst out laughing. Lance looked at Shari and smiled. "I feel like a broken horse, but I love that name." And he exploded into laughter.

"You are so stoned," Juanita said.

Lance nodded and smiled. He looked at Shari and sent her love through his eyes. "I'm sorry. I'm sorry for all of this."

Duane and Juanita stopped. Shari froze. Lance was surprised he'd spoken his thoughts.

"Sweetie," she said and moved towards him.

As stoned as he was, he heard himself speaking. "I'm so sorry I've done this to you." Hot tears started to fall. "I'm sorry you might never get to be a mother with me. I've shown up wounded. And I did it all to myself for the wrong person and it hurts you now. You're sleepwalking now, baby, and it just kills me."

She came towards him and their tears started to fall together. He held out his hands and took hers. All the words he had wanted to say those nights as he waited for her to come home poured out. "I hate myself and what we've become. I never even got to see pictures of you when you were a little girl or when you were growing up, and, uh, I," he swallowed hard. "I hate that because the truth is I want to have a little girl with you so she can look just like you did growing up and... and... she can have your hair and your little hands and feet. I want to hear how you laughed when you were little and, uh, I want all of us to sleep on our bed together in each other's arms and I just don't feel like a man anymore. I'm so scared you're going to leave me and take your love away and we'll never have what you want... I just want...." It felt like he was trying to swallow his own Adam's apple.

"I want to protect you but I did this to you before we even met. I feel like a ghost. I just don't know what to do with what I've, uh, what I've done." He wiped his eyes. "I'm just so fucking lost right now, you know? I really need you to know how sorry I am." Then he looked at her. "I feel worse than your ex who broke your jaw."

Duane and Juanita bowed their heads at this.

"I feel like I've hurt you worse than he did." Lance's tears stopped and his body racked itself with sobs. She sat down beside him and rocked him in her arms. The bag of peas was soft now, and he was stoned but he meant it. He meant it all.

She kissed his face. She kissed his tears. "I know, sweetie. I know. I know how sorry you are. But you've got to get well, okay? Whatever this infection is, you've got to get well. Why didn't you say this before? This is what I've been needing you to say."

He nodded. And she kissed his forehead. She wiped her tears away and reached for a paper towel and handed it to him. He wiped his tears and blew his nose and realized that it was the paper towel that held his former hash brownie. His nose was filled with chocolate and fudge. It was lovely. He looked to the kitchen. Juanita and Duane were hugging, rocking themselves together gently. *They're beautiful together*, he thought.

"Sorry, you guys," Lance said. "I feel like such a shit."

"It's cool, you guys. Spend the night if you want."

"No," Shari said, wiping her eyes. "I want him home." She stood and reached for Lance. "Let's go, hon."

As he reached for her hand, Lance looked up and saw her glowing. She smiled at him. And in her eyes was pride. Pride for him and what he had just said. "This," he could hear their counsellor say, "is what a courageous conversation feels like."

In the car, Lance slept for most of the way. The T3s knocked him out. He'd popped two for the pain and three ibuprofens for the swelling before they left. As he woke, they'd passed Steveston, the Massey tunnel, the Oak Street Bridge, and they were now on Marine Drive. They had a few minutes down Main Street and then they'd be at the apartment. There was no music or radio, and Lance woke to the peace that he would sleep without any arguments or silent treatment. He felt good. He felt lighter, somehow. He leaned his head against the cold window and inhaled the aroma of leftovers that Juanita insisted they take. Shari was quiet. He wasn't sure if it was because he'd finally cried or if it was because he'd finally said what he'd needed to say or if it was the hash, but he was exhausted emotionally. He leaned his head against the cold window and drifted. "What was his name again?"

Shari stared straight ahead. "Who?"

"The ball."

"Ah *you*. Nelson Crummy," she said and dragged the y out with her beautiful northern accent. "You like that, hey?"

"I do." He grinned, pleased that they were connecting again. "You know how much I love your voice."

That was another thing about Shari he'd noticed the first time he had met her: she had the most soothing voice. He loved to talk to her on the phone. It was kind, generous. A voice that was up for anything. When they had first met, she told him a story about a friend of hers who was half Ojibwa and half black. The term she explained, and the way she pronounced it drove him crazy with desire. She over-enunciated so it sounded like, "Muck-a-day-wee-ah" with a quick break at the end. He had grown immediately and fully fascinated with the way she said it. Even though her jaw had healed correctly, there were still words she could not pronounce fully. Lance had always had a weakness for anyone with a lisp, but the way she said, "Muck-a-day-wee-ah" was his Kryptonite. He'd get weak and shivery the way she said it and, one night, as they made love, he asked her to whisper the word into his ear over and over. She loved it as much as he did, and, here, this enchantment was back.

Lance looked at the eagle feather hanging from Shari's rear view mirror. He remembered their first night together, cuddling on his bed, falling asleep together. She'd fallen asleep first and turned towards him. He'd listened to her breathe, thanking his lucky stars because his wish to hold her had come true and that morning, after she left, that very morning, he'd found an eagle feather on the beach when he walked alone thinking about her and he'd given it to her on their one-month anniversary. How she treasured it, how she'd held it over her heart in astonishment. Lance had beaded a sheath of yellow, red, black and white beads for the stem.

Shari was Dene; he was Dogrib. Two hundred years ago, they would have been traditional enemies led by the Chipewyan leader, Akaitcho, and the Dogrib headman, Edzo. Lance dragged his teeth gently up Shari's back and recounted that he had betrayed the Dogribs by kidnapping her and falling in love with her, and she loved to listen to him tell elaborate stories about the love affair in their previous life together. He'd whisper as he breathed lightly into the lunar orbits in the small of her back that she was once Akaitcho's daughter and that he was Edzo's son. And as the Dogrib and Chipewyan tribes fought, they'd sneak away from each other's camps at night to make love. He whispered that they could not help themselves and that their spirit helpers, two white wolves, would warn them when scouts were approaching.

She placed her hand on his lap. "Thank you for saying what you said at the party. I really needed that, you know?" She grew quiet. "Can we talk about this in the morning? We need to talk about this."

"I want to give you everything you're asking for. You know that, hey?" He wanted to reach for her hand but his body still felt so heavy.

"I know," she squeezed his knee softly. "I know this is very hard for you." She paused. "I've been pretty hard on you, hey?"

Lance sniffled. "I've just felt so rejected. And I am scared that this is what the rest of our life together is going to be like, and you don't deserve this, sweetie. You don't. I love you so much and you've never sleepwalked before and it's because of me, you know? I keep praying those tests are wrong. I keep praying that this infection is my body's way of fighting… or—clearing the tubes."

Richard Van Camp

She nodded and sighed. "You've done all you can physically. But you did stop talking to me, Lance. I really needed to hear those words tonight." She raised and kissed the back of his hand.

Lance looked at her and saw how tired she looked. "Did you get stoned tonight?"

She shook her head. "No. I didn't take anything."

"Why?"

"I just didn't feel like it."

"Duane and Juanita didn't have any either, hey?"

"No. They had wine, but that was it."

The hash brownie party, he realized, had been for him—to bring relief, to relax him. He was humbled. Lance nodded. He could feel her sorrow. "Remember how I asked before I left if there was any chance of the reversal taking care of itself, and he said that it was one in a million?"

"No."

"I asked. I asked him. Maybe you were already in the hall but I asked him and he said it was one in a million."

"One in a million?"

"He said it was one in a million. I know you don't want to talk about adoption, but... if you want to start talking about a sperm donor...." He couldn't finish.

"A what?"

"A sperm donor. I was looking into it."

"Oh, Lance!" she said and hugged him. "I can't believe you!"

"What?" he said. "Baby, if you want to, I'd consider it."

"Lance Charlie," she said. "I want your baby. I want to bring your son or daughter into the world through my body. Any doctor who says pregnancy is one percent pregnancy and ninety-nine percent the rest of your life has his head up his ass, and I want your baby. I want you and your beautiful balls to give me what I want so I can be your wife and the mother of our children." She burst out laughing. "I love you, Lance. I love you and only you. I don't want a life of wondering ahead of us. I want us. I want us. I want us." She started to kiss his face.

Lance smiled and sank into her kisses. She had not been this affectionate in forever. "My beautiful balls?" he said. "I like the sound of this."

"Baby, I love your balls. They're smooth and they're all mine and I have been praying for them for months in the sweat and in ceremony. Do you know we have a prayer circle for your balls right now?"

"What!"

"Yes," she nodded. "There are women you have never met—aunties and grannies—praying for your beautiful balls. They are praying and dropping tobacco for them to heal properly so we can have a baby."

"Jesus!" Lance said.

"Sweetie, there is no sweeter sound to me in this life than your balls slapping against me as we make love."

Lance burst out laughing. "Holy shit! Are you frickin' stoned, or what?"

"No," she said. "I'm in love with you and I'm just so sad to see you like this. Thank God you got stoned tonight because we've been worried about you. You're getting too skinny. I don't want to cuddle up to a little bag of antlers. You've got to get strong. You're going to need your strength for our future. I won't give up on you, but don't you dare give up on our dream, okay?"

"Holy shit," Lance said again. "I'm the luckiest guy in the fuckin' world, you know that?"

"Yes you are," she said. "You think I drank all that stink tea and ate all that rabbit for nothing?"

Lance burst out laughing. *Stink tea.* That was what Shari called it every morning when they had to drink it together. She'd plug her nose and wretch as she chugged it. Part of the acupuncture and fertility treatments was to drink a Chinese tea and eat foods like rabbit. There was a theory that rabbits could get pregnant when they were pregnant so eating them would promote fertility. They also were to eat a lot of seeds, so they ate spits, sesame and hemp seeds with just about everything.

"Now let's get home," She said and drove back into the street.

My beautiful balls, he thought. *Goddamned straight they're beautiful*! He loved this! It had been so long since he felt adored. He wanted to make love to Shari and pull her close and vanish with the smell of her with the gentle brushing of his thumb against the smooth skin of her tummy. He wanted a daughter. Lance realized over the past year that a daughter was his secret wish. He wanted a little version of Shari. He wanted to see Shari holding their baby, her eyes saying, "Look at what we did. Look at what we've created together." He could see the picture. He'd place it in their first photo album as parents. Shari had created twelve photo albums that were displayed proudly in their living room. All twelve of those albums contained photos taken of them as a couple in love, as a couple with hope. They were gorgeous photos highlighting their journey together, but her photography had stopped since his reversal. Lance realized that she had not taken a single picture since the cold panic moved into their home. She patted his knee before taking the steering wheel. "We're just about home. Let's talk in the morning."

"Can we go for a walk on the beach?"

"Tomorrow?" she smiled. "Are you up for walking?"

He nodded. "I want to. I want to with you. Even if I hobble around. I want to see you in the wind."

"Okay," she said.

"I'm sorry you lost all your photos. I'm sorry about the house fire. Thank God you were all okay."

"You've never forgotten that story, hey? That's sweet of you."

"It's sad, hon. I can't imagine it. But you know, when you were telling that story, I could see you. Like, I could see you in flashes. You growing up. You becoming such a beautiful woman. I loved it, sweetie. I did."

She was quiet. He could feel her listening.

"Can I make you breakfast tomorrow?"

She laughed. "You may."

"Would you like it before or after your massage?"

"My massage?" She smiled. "I need one. Wait. Let's talk about this doorway thing of yours."

He smiled. "Not now. I'm still stoned. I adore your feet, sweetie. Remember how you used to sweep your hair all over my body? You used to take me to heaven and back with that. And I'm not sure if you read the headline in the paper today but your nipples wanted me to know that they missed my constant and loving attention." She let out a little laugh but she knew it was true. "Sweetie," he said. "The truth is you look fantastic with short hair. Can you let me massage your feet tomorrow after our walk?"

"You may."

Lance brushed the back of his hand gently against her cheek, where it had once been shattered by her ex. "What was his name again?"

"Who?"

"The soccer ball."

"Nelson Crummy," she said as if playfully annoyed.

He nodded and smiled. "One more time."

"Nelson Crummy."

He felt warmth spread again through his thighs, through his tubes, through his scars. "Sweetie, I just love the way you say it. I've always loved your voice." His acupuncturist told him every session to imagine a clearing blue light pouring through him, to travel up his body and to blast through anything that blocked his chakras, tubes and spirit. He'd tried but every time he did, the light was green. Now, now it was blue and it poured through every artery, every vein, every passage with the speaking of the soccer ball's name.

"I love you," he said. "With everything. I am so proud to be your man."

"I love you, too," she said. "I'm glad you got stoned tonight. I've been hard on you, hey?"

He started to feel a freeze up so he nodded slowly. *Speak through it,* he thought. *Don't freeze.* "Baby?" They pulled into their parking lot and Lance held up his left hand. "Can I tell you a secret?"

She turned the car off and turned to him. "Is it about cumming in doorways?"

He grinned. "No. It's a secret and it's only for you. I've never told you this before."

He pointed to his left hand, to the cup of his palm. "This is my second favourite place in the world."

"I don't get it."

"That first night I met you, like really met you, you were a consideration."

Her voice became guarded. "A consideration?"

Lance nodded. "Well, you and I were aware of each other. You were seeing what's-his-name."

She pushed his arm gently. "Yeah, yeah. Go on."

"Well, you'd come back from the bar and you were sipping coffee and it smelled great. It was midnight and you'd just finished singing. You stood by me. There were no other places to sit, so you stood beside me."

"I remember."

"You stood by me and you were coming back from getting another coffee and I wanted to smell it on your breath. It was fresh. You came by and I turned. I turned to ask you about the night, the band, where the gang was going, and I decided to place my hand on your hip. It was just the way we were standing. And I touched your hip, and you were so soft. I was cupping you with my left hand and you leaned into me and you even placed your hand on my shoulder. You answered me. You were holding your coffee and as we spoke you moved. You were moving to the music and I could feel your hips, the muscle, the softness of your skin underneath your shirt and then we got separated. The gang went one way. I had to go to work early. But when I went to bed that night, my hand was burning with how smooth you were. You and I have always been aware of each other. I'd been checking you out for months."

"Stalker," she grinned. "Checking me out for months, hey?"

He nodded. "Yeah. Sweetie, I went to bed and wondered about you. I wondered why the hell hadn't we dated? I mean, there were times you and I were single at the same time. But I went to bed and when I woke up and my hand was still burning with the memory and the wonder of what was beneath. I drove. I remember I had to work in Abbotsford the next day and I'd look at my hand, where I'd cupped your hip and it was burning. It burned for a week until I saw you again and that was when I made my move."

"You mean when I let you make your move."

Lance nodded. He took her hand in his and kissed it. "Here's what I've never told you. When I went for my reversal—"

"You touched me there again," she said. "I wondered about that. You did it before you went under."

Lance nodded. "I did. And when I woke up I asked for you."

"And you did it again," she said. "It was the first place you touched." Lance saw a single tear fall down her face, surprising them both.

"To this very day," he said, he could feel tears well. "I have never stopped feeling you in this hand." He looked to his open palms. "I never told you this, but I'm magic."

She laughed. "And stoned."

"No," he said. "No. I'm serious. You know my grandparents were medicine people, too, and that they never spoke a word of English. I wish you could have met them. They would have loved you. Treasured you."

She whispered, "I'm sorry I didn't, sweetie. I know you miss them."

He nodded. Lance had been raised by his grandparents. His own parents were alcoholics who refused to change. They weren't close at all. Getting a vasectomy was about not passing on what he had been born into, and this is why he didn't drink. "I do. You know, when I was growing up, there's a lot you still don't know about me, I was looking forward. I mean… I had this idea that I could spend the rest of my life telling you and showing you how magic I am."

He looked to her. She glanced at him. "Go on."

"And I just trusted that you would spend the rest of your life with me, astonishing me with all the little things you do without even knowing."

She smiled.

"When I was a kid. Every Canada Day we used to go out to Pine Lake. Remember when I took you there?"

She pushed his arm, playfully. They'd had the whole beach to themselves, and in broad daylight on a picnic table on sand the colour of cinnamon, he'd gone down on her over and over all afternoon, drinking her, lapping her and making love to her only with his tongue, breath and lips. She'd been astonished at how hungry he was for her and she was both exhausted and speechless with how wonderful it was, to have him between her thighs, him knowing exactly what to do and her looking up to clouds as white as snow, the sky so blinding in blue. She smiled. "Go on."

"We used to go on these expeditions called bison creeps," he said. "You can't do this now. But back then, we used to go in the bush and we'd creep towards the bison. Our parents and elders used to wait on the highway in their trucks and I was like seven or eight. There'd be about forty of us. And what we'd do is we'd move slowly with the shadows towards the herd. There'd be fifty to a hundred bison in the shade, and we'd move with the sun to take the fur that they'd rubbed off onto the bark of the trees. The game was whoever could grab the fur on the trees closest to the herd and make it back to the elders without disturbing the bison would be the winner. You'd have bragging rights for a whole year."

She laughed. "How would they know who won?"

"They watched from their trucks, using binoculars."

"Your parents let you do this?"

He winced at the memory. "My parents never knew: they were drinking at the Pine Crest or sleeping it off at home. It was the way boys became men. It was a ritual for the town. I loved the way the fur smelled. I can still smell it sometimes when I miss home. I felt like a wolf."

She ran her hand over his arm. "Wow."

Lance nodded. "One year, I really wanted to win. I did this thing where I moved with the sun. I wasn't going to leave until I knew I won. I had bathed myself in the smoke of the fire in our backyard, and I hadn't eaten buffalo meat in ten days. I was dead serious about winning. I had dropped tobacco, and I even asked that we pray together for a week before the event."

"*Ho-la*," she said. "I'll never make fun of Fort Smith again. Go on."

"Well, I did this thing where I moved so slowly and I prayed to my grandparents. This was when they were still with us. I prayed to them, and I did this thing where I put myself in my own back pocket as I moved, my spirit, I mean. And I moved within the shadows and I knew other kids were turning back, so I had to move in closer. I moved in closer and, as I moved, I could hear my heartbeat. Soon, I heard other heartbeats, like little drums. And I realized that it was the heartbeats of the herd I was approaching. I swear to God I could hear them, feel them. And I moved. I moved and made my way. And I closed my eyes and I trusted. I don't know how long I moved so slowly but I did and I brushed up against something and it was a bull. We both jumped and he ran away, starting a stampede. I had walked into the heart of them and bumped a bull. Holy cow, you should have heard people yelling for me. They were worried I'd been trampled. I had walked right into the heart of them and had touched the biggest bull there."

"Oh my God," she said. "That's crazy."

"Yeah," he said. "And you know, as they ran away, I looked down and in my hand was a handful of fur. I had been pulling it off of his body and he didn't even know until it was too late."

She looked at him. "Are you telling the truth?"

He held his palm up and opened it. "I swear to God." He pointed to the little blue beads in the sheath he had beaded for her on their one-year anniversary. "Those seven blue beads are the heartbeats I heard in the heart of where I stood. I have not felt anything near that kind of magic until I felt you. Not only that night, but on that first night we laid together. I placed my hand on your hip as you slept and that was when I knew that I wanted everything with you: a future, a family, a home." He pointed to his palm again. "This hand is yours. I've never stopped feeling the memory of you in me. I swear. You are the most mysterious woman in the world to me, and I've never stopped thinking of ways to amaze you. I live to see you smile. I love pampering you. I do. You got me through that reversal and I did it for you."

This was tender ground and he decided to stop because the slingshot answer that often came out in therapy was, "But you got a vasectomy for her."

But she said nothing. Lance could tell that response was on her tongue. She nodded and put the keys in her purse. "Thank you."

He took her hand and kissed her palm. "I'm sorry it took me so long to find you."

She kissed his palm. "Oh, sweetie. Thank you. Thank you for saying this. Do you know how long I've been waiting to hear you say something?"

"I'm just so scared sometimes you'll leave me when I've just realized that I want to be a father, and I want to see you as a mother. I'd love to be parents with you and I never felt safe enough with Larissa to ever even think like this before or wish for a family but with you I know I found the right wolf to run with."

She smiled, astonished at his sweetness. "Well, words like those will always hold me close. So keep talking, okay? You're a storyteller, but that is different from saying what I need to hear—and from what you need to say."

He nodded. "I promise."

● ○ ●

The next morning there was breakfast, and Lance went all out. Even though the swelling was tender, most of his pain was gone. Shari's ancestors were chanters, she once told him. Maybe the way she said Nelson Crummy was a chant that had begun to work on him. "Nelson Crummy, Nelson Crummy, Nelson Crummy," he said. "Virility, virility, virility." He made his Spanish omelettes; he made her coffee just the way she liked it, and he cut up fresh fruit for her. He even made them a smoothie for their expedition. He had three cups of coffee himself as celebration of their big breakthrough as a couple. We're back! he quietly celebrated. He went outside and dropped tobacco in gratitude for the new day before them.

After, they shared a slow walk along Kits beach, stopping for tea and muffins, watching the Vancouverites enjoying the day and each other. Then a careful shower. Lance surrendered to the bliss and warmth of her tummy against his as he soaped her body from head to toe. The kissing through hot water, the losing himself into her body where his body became hers was theirs once again. When they used to make love, Shari would run her fingers through his hair over and over, as she grew close to climax.

"I want you," Lance said.

Shari brushed her nipples across his. "Are you sure?"

"Baby, yes," he said.

"Be careful, okay?"

"Promise."

They unplugged the phones, shut the blinds to the house. Lance provided an hour-long body rub and foot massage using coconut oil. He made her moan and took her toes into his mouth. He devoured them with kisses and moaned as he licked with playful nibbles around them. It was delicious. She bucked and writhed in delight at his skill and, after, there was gentle pampering using massage, breath and tongue. He was still too sore to have sex but Shari orgasmed twice and was thrilled with how much she missed him, missed *them*.

As they lay together, her back against his chest, he breathed into the nape of her neck. He pulled her close in his strong arms.

"What was his name again?" he whispered.

She closed her eyes. "What?"

"Tell me his name."

"Whose name?"

"The soccer ball."

She smiled and let out a long sigh. "Nelson Crummy."

She felt him grin against her back. He hugged her lovingly, pulling her into him. Her nipples ached, ready for attention, as the tips of her ears and the heels of her feet were burning from his massage. He'd gone deep and she'd surrendered to the pampering, pushing the worry and grief away. She was thrilled with his hunger to please her again but worried he was still too tender to make love to.

But he was so hungry for her today. "I see you. I see you growing up. Keep going. What was his name?"

She giggled. "Nelson Crummy." And she said it as if it was exhausting her.

"I see you. You're growing up and you've got big hair, and then short hair, and then a great perm and then a bad one." She laughed. "What was his name?"

"Baby," she said as if she was too fatigued.

He kissed her neck and feathered his thumb across her nipple. "Please, baby, just tell me. I can see you when you tell that story."

He ground himself into her from behind and he started kissing her neck, where he knew it drove her crazy. She turned and rolled into him. They were naked and it felt so good to touch tummy-to-tummy, nipple to nipple. Lance smelled of coconut. She licked the taste of herself off his lips and felt the hot bloom of blood beneath her throat spread like a sunset under her skin. Her breasts began to ache for touch, nuzzling and kiss—in only the way he could adore them. Each time for them was like the first time for him. He trembled and shivered every time they made love, and she enjoyed seducing him with her power, her strength.

"Want me to say it again?" she whispered and placed her leg over his hip so she could feel his heat brush her sex with a whisper.

He placed his hand there, in that magic spot. "Please."

"Whose name?"

"The angel at your table."

She smiled and took her time, whispering into his ear. "Nelson Crummy. Nelson Crummy. Nelson Crummy."

He could hear her little sharp breaths at the end of every time she said it and he became weak. "Oh, baby," he said. He kissed her and gently brushed himself against her. She carefully used her leg to pull him closer. She could feel his body heat caress her sex and she curled her toes. "Say it again. Say it over and over."

"I'm healing you and it's Nelson Crummy."

"Oh," he started to shiver and groan. "Oh, baby." He gripped her hips harder.

"His name was Nelson Crummy. Can you see me?"

She started to kiss Lance's face and his eyes were closed in complete trust.

"Baby, I can."

She could feel him against her. "Be careful, sweetie. Don't hurt yourself. What do you see?"

"I see you. Growing up. Laughing and trusting. I see you, baby. I see you." And suddenly Lance was inside her, gently. Just the head of him and she was wet and ready. She was surprised that she was soaked and Lance was inside her now. "Tell me," he said. "Baby, tell me his name."

She took him inside her and was amazed to feel how hot and hard he was. They hadn't made love in months and here they were. She took him, and they were together, and she needed this. She needed Lance inside her. Lance started to kiss her neck and he glided inside her, carefully, slowly.

Richard Van Camp

He gripped her ankle, his favourite thing to do when he was close and she said, "Baby, I love you and his name was Nelson Crummy," and that was when Lance burst inside of her. He came in such a rush that neither of them was prepared, and he filled her with himself. She cried out in both surprise and delight as she took all of him. She took all of him and felt something inside her she'd never felt before. She felt a blue searing light spread sweetly from her thighs into her tummy, and she suddenly felt a light fill her womb. Her eyes opened in shock. *My womb*, she thought. She'd never said those words before. A light filled her womb and her body heaved to catch all of it and gather it inside her, into herself, into her life, into her future, and it was everything she'd asked for, everything they deserved.

"Baby," he pulled her close. "Oh, baby. Did you feel us?"

She took his hands and pulled them towards her heart as she backed into him. She smiled. *We have fallen back into ourselves,* she thought. As heat and light found them both, Shari suddenly burst into tears. "Yes."

AFTERWORDS

While individual stories are dedicated to those who inspired them, I'd like to dedicate the spirit of this collection to my family, my elders, my teachers, my students, and all my dear friends who are the family of my heart. You know who you are. *Mahsi cho* for believing in me and for all your inspiration. You are good medicine to me, and I am grateful to all of you.

I'd like to thank my editor, Maurice Mierau, my publisher, Gregg Shilliday, my dear friend, Anita Daher, and Catharina de Bakker at Enfield & Wizenty for believing in this collection so strongly right from the beginning. *Mahsi cho*!

"Show Me Yours" first appeared in *The Walrus* (November, 2007). This story is dedicated to northerners everywhere—especially in Yellowknife and Fort Smith, NWT. I'd like to say a huge *mahsi cho* to Jennifer Knowlan for being there when the story found me. Jennifer and I were walking out of the Wildcat Café in

Yellowknife and I asked, "Hey, what if everyone started wearing their baby pictures around their necks? Wouldn't that be magic?" As well, I'd like to say a huge *mahsi cho* to Jim Northrup for his writing and storytelling. His story "Goose Goose" in *Walking the Rez Road* is one of my all time favourites and that same spirit of community and humor definitely inspired me to write this story. *Mahsi cho*, Jim!

"NDNs" was originally published in the Fall 2009 issue of the *Canadian Journal of Native Studies*. I'd like to dedicate "NDNs" to my brother, Jamie, and to the memory of my grandmother, Melanie Wah-shee, and especially to my mother, Rosa.

"Dogrib Midnight Runners" was published in *Up Here Magazine* in 2006. This story was inspired by the life of Paul Grundy and I'd like to dedicate this to his memory, his family, his friends, to everyone in Fort Smith and to streakers everywhere!

"Love Walked In" is dedicated to Trevor Evans, Chris Labonte, Bob Tyrrell, Luke Oskirko and Garth Prosper and to the women in my life who keep me strong: Chantal Rondeau, Katrina Chappell, Julie Lees, Stephanie Winch, Karen V. Bowers, Erin Macdonald, Tracy D. Smith, Loretta Seto, Christina Piovesan, Anita Doron, Renate Eigenbrod, Leigh-Anne Mercier, Leanne Padgett, Kateri Akiwenzie-Damm, Renee K. Abram, Jennifer Duncan, Jamie Therrien, Kym Gouchie, Jenny Simpson, Janice Forsey, Judith Drinnan, Barbie Everett, Zoe Ballentyne, Amy Reiswig, Trika Macdonald, Helena Krobath, Kelly Kitchen, and Keavy Martin.

"The Last Snow of the Virgin Mary" was published in *Moccasin Thunder*, edited by Lori Mari Carlson (HarperCollins, 2005). I'd like to dedicate this story to my brothers Roger Wah-shee and Johnny Van Camp as well as Mike Mahussier, Jon Liv Jaque, James Croizier, Dusty Kamps, Trevor Evans, Junior Mercredi, Sean Muir, and Trevor Cameron.

I'd like to dedicate "The Moon of Letting Go" to the memory of Snowbird Martin, the late great Melvin Greybear, and to my late grandfather, Pierre Wah-shee.

"I Count Myself Among Them" was published in the Summer 2009 issue of *Prairie Fire*. I want to acknowledge Andris Taskans and Heidi Harms at *Prairie Fire* for publishing two of the stories in this collection. I've always admired *Prairie Fire* for its commitment to publishing brilliant Canadian literature and it is an honour to be included in their magnificence. I would like to dedicate this story to all the artists I adore who welcomed me into the full grace of the blood in men: my dad, Roger Brunt, my father, Jack Van Camp, Craig Lesley, Sherman Alexie, Robert Arthur Alexie, Harold Hoefle, Michael Bryson, Barry Lopez, Sarain Stump, Adrian C. Louis, N. Scott Momaday, Richard Wagamese, Geary Hobson, Daniel Heath Justice, Warren Cariou, Bill Valgardson, Patrick Lane, Pat Conroy, Daniel Woodrell, James Welch, Alootook Ippellie, The Mission, The Cure, The Sisters of Mercy, The Ministry, CircleSquare, Placebo, Fields of the Nephilim, A Perfect Circle, She Wants Revenge, Dead Can Dance, Nick Tosches, Steve Sanderson, Steven "Jesse" Bernstein, Garry Gottfriedson, Joseph Dandurand, Gregory Scofield, Chris Bose, Billeh Nickerson, Joseph Boyden, Drew Hayden Taylor, Kent Williams, George Littlechild, Francois Paulette, Thomas King, Niigonwedom James Sinclair, Chris Paul and Marty Ballentyne who gave me the title for this dream without even knowing it. As well, I'd like to acknowledge Stan Bourke and his family for this story.

"Don't Forget This" was published in the anthology *Stories from Moccasin Avenue* (Totem Pole Books). This story was inspired by a time in my life when I lived in Penticton attending the En'owkin International School of Writing and I'd like to dedicate this story to my En'owkin family. I'd also like to acknowledge the master storytellers in my life who have inspired me in everything that I do: Ivan Coyote, Lee Maracle, Jeannette Armstrong, Glen Douglas, Henry Jenson, Irene Sanderson, Maria Brown, Roberta Kennedy, Seraphine Evans, Edna Beaver, Nora Doig, Sharon Shorty, Earl and Marlene Evans, George Blondin, Winston Wuttunee, Norman Hall, Dr. Lee Brown, and everyone else I have had the honour of listening to and learning from.

"The Power of Secrets" was published in the UBC Alumni *Trek Magazine* (Spring, 2008). I'd like to dedicate this story to everyone in Bella Bella/ Waglisla and to Trevor Evans.

I'd like to dedicate "Wolf Medicine: A Ceremony of You" to Gudrun Will and Mark Mushet from the *Vancouver Review* for honouring the wish and spirit of this story so wonderfully in their Winter 2007 issue with a pictorial by Mark Mushet featuring models Helen Haig-Brown and D'Arcy O'Connor. This song was hand sculpted to one song on repeat hundreds of times: "Spiders" by System of a Down. I saw this story through this song. *Mahsi cho*, System of a Down!

"Idioglossia" was originally published as "Dypthia" in *Prairie Fire* (Autumn, 2001), edited by Thomas King, whom I'd like to thank for believing in me right from the get-go. I'd like to dedicate this story to John Beder who told me about the secret, bird-like and haunting language of two brother twins he knew.

I'd like to dedicate "A Darling Story" to Anna Swanson who told me about Nelson Crummy and sent me on my way with a dare and a deadline. I'd also like to dedicate this story to every couple out there facing fertility issues. *Be strong and gentle together.* I'd also like to thank Dana Claxton for commissioning this story for the Good Medicine Project with the Grunt Gallery. As well, I'd like to thank Kateri Akiwenzie-Damm for editing the story and Annelies Pool for being such a great first reader and dear friend.

"Dogrib Midnight Runners," "Show Me Yours," "NDNs," and "The Power of Secrets" were narrated and broadcast on CBC Radio One when I was North by Northwest's Writer in Residence in 2007. You can hear them on the Enfield & Wizenty website at www.enfieldandwizenty.ca and on mine at www.richardvancamp.org. I'd like to thank Sheryl MacKay for being such a great producer and editor during this golden time of creation and narration.

Mahsi cho! Thank you for reading these stories. They have taken me many lifetimes in this one to dream and share.